Krammin' With A Kraken

Slaymore Academy - Book 1

**Sedona Ashe writing as Darci R. Acula**

**Starling Dax**

Copyright © 2023 by Sedona Ashe

Gobble Ink, LLC

This is a work of fiction. Names, characters, places, and incidents either are the product of the author's imagination or are used fictitiously. Any resemblance to actual persons, living or dead, events, or locales is entirely coincidental.

www.sedonaashe.com

All rights reserved. No part of this book may be reproduced or used in any manner without written permission of the copyright owner except for the use of quotations in a book review. For more information, address: sedonaashe@gmail.com

*Cover artwork by Alex Calder*

*www.addictivecovers.com*

Interior artwork by Cauldron Press

*www.cauldronpress.ca*

A huge thank you to-

Allison Woerner for Alpha Reading.

Maxine Meyer for Copy Editing.

Imogen Evans for Proofreading & Editing.

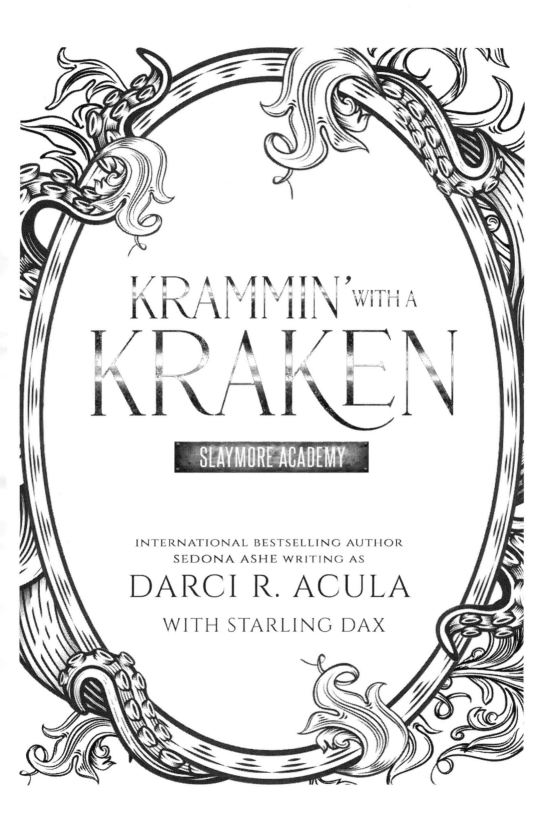

# KRAMMIN' WITH A KRAKEN

## SLAYMORE ACADEMY

INTERNATIONAL BESTSELLING AUTHOR
SEDONA ASHE WRITING AS

# DARCI R. ACULA

WITH STARLING DAX

*Sensitivity Note*
*Warning: spoilers below!*

*The female in this book is a kraken. This means when shifted, she does possess tentacles. And boy, oh boy, does she know how to use them… in probably the same way you'd use tentacles if you had them (yes, I'm talking about YOU!). If you aren't into creativity and steam in the bedroom, and other places, then you should probably skip this book. There is bullying from one student who isn't cool with krakens, but he is not her mate!*

CONTENTS

| | |
|---|---:|
| Chapter One | 1 |
| Chapter Two | 9 |
| Chapter Three | 25 |
| Chapter Four | 41 |
| Chapter Five | 57 |
| Chapter Six | 67 |
| Chapter Seven | 81 |
| Chapter Eight | 91 |
| Chapter Nine | 101 |
| Chapter Ten | 119 |
| Chapter Eleven | 133 |
| Chapter Twelve | 149 |
| Chapter Thirteen | 163 |
| Chapter Fourteen | 173 |
| Chapter Fifteen | 181 |
| Chapter Sixteen | 197 |
| Chapter Seventeen | 203 |
| Chapter Eighteen | 213 |
| Chapter Nineteen | 225 |
| Chapter Twenty | 237 |
| Chapter Twenty-one | 251 |
| | |
| *About Darci R. Acula* | 255 |
| *About Starling Dax* | 257 |

## CHAPTER I
### SETA

"We're here, miss."

My hired car pulled to a stop on the wide gravel drive. I stared out the window at the mansion before me, running my fingers along the cool gold of the cuff at my left wrist. Slaymore Academy of the Supernatural—my home for the next four years.

The driver who'd brought me from port to academy opened the door and helped me out with a gloved hand. He'd barely said two words to me on the drive, but that was more than okay with me.

Small talk was nonsense, and I didn't do nonsense. But judging by the over-the-top appearance of Slaymore, the headmasters must be fine with nonsense.

The Slaymore mansion looked like a giant layer cake made of pale stone. The house was square, more or less, but towers and stories had been added to it in a hodgepodge fashion.

These additions stuck out at crazy angles from the outer walls. There were also smaller towers sprouting from larger towers in a way that made me suspect magic had been involved in the construction.

Each sprawling floor had a balcony running around it, which was supported at odd intervals by intricately carved stone pillars. Ivy crawled up a few walls and curled around the pillars on the ground floor of the house. I had to admire its tenacity. It knew where it wanted to be, just like I did.

The lawn in front of the mansion burst with springy grass, and several students lounged on it, with books and guitars scattered around them.

A mermaid sat with her fluke dangling in a marble fountain that featured a concrete dragon with wings out and neck extended to attack. Instead of fire, water sprayed from her jaws.

The sight of the clear, sparkling water tugged at my heart and stirred the magic in my center. I touched my cuff again, reassuring myself of its presence. As long as I wore the cuff, I would only reveal myself if I wanted to.

Still, it was best that I stayed away from water for now.

The driver set my suitcase down, and I thanked him with a few folded twenties. He tipped his hat, and his shoes crunched on the white gravel drive as he went back to the driver's seat. A moment later, he pulled away.

And with that, reality set in.

This was happening.

## KRAMMIN' WITH A KRAKEN

I was landlocked at Slaymore.

Tendrils of panic tried to curl around my stomach, but I clamped down on them. I wasn't the type to get anxious. Panic was definitely nonsense, and I didn't have time for that.

Taking a breath, I ran through the plan in my head again: *Go to Slaymore, get my degree in Marine Mythology, go back to the Deep where I belong. Be studious, polite, and upstanding.*

Those were my orders. Well, and *find a mate,* but I had every intention of ignoring that last marching order from my mother. At twenty, I was too young to bind my life to someone else, no matter how dire she claimed the situation was at home.

I checked the pocket of my jacket. Yep, it was still there —the official letter accepting my attendance at Slaymore and documents that declared my status as an ambassador for the Bering Kraken clan.

Now that I'd checked off point one—*Go to Slaymore*—I had to present these papers to the headmistress. I was guessing she must have been in her office somewhere in the enormous funhouse in front of me.

"Hey!" Feet sounded on the drive behind me.

I flinched. It was hard getting used to the way things sounded above water. Turning, I came face-to-face with the most beautiful creature I'd ever seen.

His burnished skin seemed to radiate light. It was as though he'd captured the sun and refracted it, just like the warm afternoon light that shimmered across the surface of the ocean.

Golden hair curled in a gentle halo around his head, and his face was a study in strong lines. He had a sturdy, clean-shaven jaw, a proud nose, and eyes as blue as the Aegean Sea.

I stepped back to let him run past, assuming he'd seen a friend behind me, but the guy stopped… *right in front of me.*

"Hey," he said again. He wore a blue T-shirt with *SLAYMORE* written across the front, and his mouth parted with a flash of white teeth that nearly had me reaching for my sunglasses. "New here? Looking for Headmistress Losia?"

"Uh…" My thoughts felt like they were trapped in honey.

Was my sudden flush of warmth because of *him* or the heat of the sunny day? His voice was so gentle, a rumbling presence that reminded me of the gentle giants of the sea.

"Who are you?" I quickly covered my mouth. This time, my flush was from pure mortification.

The guy just laughed and stuck out his hand. "Amadeus. My friends call me Deus."

"Hi, De!" trilled the mermaid from the fountain.

He waved at her, then added, "Or you can call me De."

I shook his hand. Human palms were so dry, and his was warm; it was hardly the smooth, scaly greeting I was used to.

*Well, you're going to have to get used to a lot of new things,* I reminded myself. But making friends didn't have to be one of them.

My mother's voice sounded sharp in my head. *If you want any sort of mate, you'll have to find him there.*

Right. She'd been very clear about what *her* biggest goal for my life was.

I pulled my hand away and tucked it behind my back. Mom might have sent me to Slaymore with the hope of me finding a mate, but that wasn't why I'd agreed to come.

I was here to get my degree and get out.

Guys were just another type of nonsense and a distraction from my real goal. I was here to become a scholar of Marine Mythology.

Oh, and also to prove to the world that Krakens were civilized shepherds of the ocean and not the monstrous killers legends made us out to be.

"Did you get your room assignment yet?" Amadeus was asking. "Roommates and first semester classes—those are the biggest things. Though if you're really into sports—"

He was still smiling… and glowing. Were all humans this bright? Or was this something special to him, to his powers? What was he?

"I'm fine," I interrupted his friendly ramble, a little more coldly than I'd intended. "I don't need anything."

That got Amadeus to stop talking, though his smile didn't falter. Why didn't he think I was rude?

He scratched the back of his neck. "When I saw the car pull up, I was curious. And, well, you looked a little lost."

"I don't need help," I mumbled.

"I'd be happy to carry your bag," he offered.

We looked down at my Samsonite suitcase. Everything

inside it I'd bought yesterday after coming ashore. Funnily enough, things that thrived in the Deep didn't do so well on dry land.

The only thing I'd brought from home was the gold cuff on my wrist that suppressed my powers and my true form. My suitcase held a week's worth of clothes and toiletries, and I could lift it with a finger.

Which I did.

"I've got it." I offered him my best shot at a smile, something that definitely needed practice, and started toward the mansion's front door.

Walking out of his sphere felt like going from day to night. The air around me seemed colder and darker, and I felt alone. But I didn't turn around, not wanting him to know he'd affected me.

Judging by the mermaid's enthusiastic greeting, Golden Boy probably had this effect on a lot of people.

"Do you know where you're going?" he called after me.

"Close enough!" I shouted over my shoulder.

Pushing on the mansion's creaking front door, I barely kept from rolling my eyes at the cliché. Cool air brushed past me.

"She's just up the stairs—" Amadeus shouted from behind me.

Stepping inside, the door closed, and his voice was silenced.

I was acting like I had a stiff tentacle up my butt, and he probably thought I was an arse. But I wasn't here to make friends, and if everyone left me alone, it would make studying easier.

And I definitely wasn't here to get married, no matter what Mom said.

Squaring my shoulders, I touched my cuff again.

*Stick to the plan,* I thought, pausing to let my eyes adjust to the dim interior.

## CHAPTER 2
### SETA

It was when I headed up the stairs that things became complicated. There were no directory signs pointing in the direction of the office. Instead, I found a seemingly endless number of hallways.

I was pretty sure I counted more hallways than rooms, and there were far more windows inside than I'd seen from the outside. Magic had definitely been involved in the building of Slaymore Academy.

I was no stranger to magic spaces—our own keep at the bottom of the ocean was heavily enchanted. But I needed to find the headmistress soon. I was still getting used to my human form, and my head was beginning to hurt from the thinness of the air.

Making my way down the hall, I peered cautiously into half a dozen rooms on the first floor before taking a creaking set of stairs up to the second. The stairwell walls were papered with a fading rose pattern that looked like it belonged in my great-grandma's sitting room.

On the second floor, I found a perfectly polished grand piano, a full suit of armor, and a fading couch. Beneath the piano bench, there was a box with a large lock and a *DO NOT OPEN* sign sitting on top of it.

Still, there was no headmistress to be found.

I made my way to the third floor. Gold-framed artwork lined both walls on either side of the hall. Whoever decorated the third floor must have really liked still-life paintings. It wasn't until I reached the end of the hall that I found any signs of life at all.

The office door hadn't been closed all the way, and squinting through the small gap, I spotted a desk at the window, a chair, and a furiously writing hand. I paused.

"Why are you lurking?" said an impatient, cracking voice from the chair.

"Headmistress Losia?" I hadn't been invited into the room, so I stood frozen in the hall.

"Do I look like Headmistress Losia to you?" the voice snarled. The writing hand scrawled something and flicked a sheet of paper away.

I had no idea what the owner of the voice looked like, but the correct answer was obvious. "No."

"Headmistress's office is on the first floor, at the end of the left fork on the far side of the dining room. Remember to tap the St. George statue as you go by; otherwise, he won't let you see it."

I tried to memorize the tangled instructions in my head. "Thank you."

"And for goodness' sake, don't forget your map next time." The angry writer muttered something about careless students as I tiptoed away from the door.

Retracing my steps, I went back down to the first floor. Finding the correct hallway, I tapped the statue and discovered a dining room I'd missed the first time around.

"Thanks, George," I muttered as I made my way across the room filled with empty wooden chairs and tables covered with light-blue tablecloths.

As I approached, the door at the end of the dining room opened. A relieved-appearing student scuttled out, clutching a pile of books and a sheet of paper that looked like it could be a map.

"The headmistress is so nice," the girl gushed as she passed me. "She gave me the last single room. That's a *serious* relief for a gorgon."

"Last single room?" I asked as she hurried away. Did that mean I was going to have to share?

The door was ajar, but I still knocked before looking in. "Head-headmistress?"

A woman with a short gray bob sat at a wide ebony desk. She looked up and smiled brightly. Behind a pair of cat-eye glasses, her eyes were a unique color that flickered between orange and red.

"You must be Seta." She stood, showing a perfectly pressed dark red suit that had been paired with a soft cream shirt.

I got a whiff of brimstone as I leaned over the desk to shake her extended hand. The headmistress' skin felt dry just as Amadeus's hand had, but hers was far scalier.

"We've been looking forward to your arrival." Her smile was warm and genuine. "It's not often Slaymore gets a new type of student these days, and we've made several special accommodations for your arrival. I believe you have the necessary paperwork?"

Nodding, I pulled the ambassadorial documents out of my pocket. Headmistress Losia flicked through them, dipping her chin in approval at each one.

"Wonderful! It all appears to be in order. Welcome to Slaymore." She gestured for me to sit. "Now, on to the elephant in the room, so to speak."

Pausing, she tilted her head as if listening for any eavesdroppers in the room outside. "Normally, I welcome students from a new... background... in my yearly welcome speech. But your case is a bit unique."

*Tell me something I don't know.* I thought the words but didn't dare say them out loud.

There were very few Kraken clans left in the world, and we were not well-loved by land dwellers. Instead of being recognized as protectors of the ocean, we were seen as man-killing, ship-sinking monsters.

Over the countless centuries, many a monster slayer had tried to make his name by killing members of my family. Heck, even the other magical beings saw Krakens as something to fear.

We could create whirlpools, tsunamis, waterspouts, and

even hurricanes. And those things tended to be all that people remembered about us.

Never mind that we spent our lives trying to stop these disasters or that we tried to shield people from the brunt of the destruction and harm.

Nope. Everyone liked to focus on the damage we *could* do if we wanted.

In fact, I'd been surprised when Headmistress Losia had written back with a letter of acceptance for Slaymore. More than one magical academy had refused my application, using the excuse of doing it 'for the safety of the student body.'

Headmistress Losia must have guessed at what was going on in my mind. Leaning forward, she patted my arm.

"Every good fight is a hard one." Her eyes held understanding and maybe a touch of sadness. "I know what it is to be where you are. And at Slaymore, we don't discriminate against *anyone*."

I nodded. Losia was a dragon, another loathed race, and the path she'd forged had helped a lot of so-called monsters gain the rights of other paranormals. I could trust her to support me and keep my secrets.

"But there are some students who come from more… traditional families. We have a couple of slayers, a few descendants from the old heroes, that sort of thing. You're listed in our database as a mermaid from outside one of the colonies, so no one will think it's odd if they catch you going for a swim. I understand that you can keep your unique powers hidden?"

I held out my left arm, and she leaned in to examine the cuff. "It works everywhere, even in seawater." There was no hiding the twinge of pride in my voice. I'd helped make it with our court armorer. "As long as I'm wearing it, I have to make the choice to release my tentacles."

"Excellent." Headmistress Losia turned back to her computer. "I'll classify it as a medical aid in your file. That will allow you to wear the bracelet at all times, even during exams and events where normal enchanted jewelry is prohibited."

Her fingers flew across her keyboard. When she finished typing, she took off her glasses and gave me a sharp look. "You do realize that keeping a secret of this nature will be daunting."

"I won't have a problem with it." This wasn't my first time visiting land, and all my life, I'd known we couldn't reveal ourselves to anyone, either human or paranormal.

Sure, I hated it. I was proud to be a kraken, a shepherd of the sea. But I understood the necessity of keeping my secret. I'd attended too many Kraken burials not to.

"I hope not. However, *should* the truth come out, as of this moment, you are an ambassador from the Bering Kraken clan. Any act of aggression against you is considered an act of aggression against the Bering paranormal community and the entire Kraken race."

Sitting back in her chair, she opened a drawer and pulled out several papers. "Now. You'll need a map, a room assignment, and your course list for the first semester." Her brow lifted, and she pinned me with a sharp stare. "Are you sitting on coals, dear?"

I'd been shifting in my seat, antsy. Taking a deep breath, I smoothed my hands on my jeans and tried to appear confident, like the ambassador I now was. "Well, actually, I was wondering… someone said there were single rooms?"

"It's our policy to give every first-year student a roommate," Headmistress Losia said with a smile. "It can feel lonely, starting at the academy, where so many students know no one. We do keep single rooms on hand for people with special considerations, but I'm afraid we gave the last one away."

"But the secretive nature of my race—" I tried.

Headmistress Losia slid her glasses down her nose. "You seemed confident you could keep that secret a few minutes ago."

She had me there. Deciding whining about it wouldn't get me anywhere since Losia seemed to dislike nonsense as much as I did. I pressed my lips together.

"Is that all?" she asked.

"Independent study," I said quickly before I could lose my nerve. "I mean. I want to… I would like to follow a course of independent study."

The headmistress was already shaking her head.

I licked my lips and tucked a strand of bright red hair behind my ear. "I have an optimal course list. I work well alone. You've seen my previous academic record—"

"You're a gifted student, Seta," Losia gently interrupted. "But life at Slaymore isn't the same as life among tutors and waitstaff. The academy is designed to give you a valuable learning experience and important life experiences. I simply can't let you take shortcuts with that. Should an individual professor grant you leave to study a subject independently, that's one thing. But I can't interfere with their courses."

My own brow wrinkled. "You're the headmistress. You can do whatever you want."

Headmistress Losia laughed at that. "All right. I *want* you to have the full Slaymore experience. A roommate, group learning, dormitory food and all."

She handed me the stack of papers she'd pulled from the drawer. "Welcome to Slaymore, Seta."

SLAYMORE'S CAMPUS consisted of much more than just the Victorian house near the front gate. As I left the house through a back door, I found myself on a massive lawn dotted with students.

A few paranormal species were obvious—vampires with parasols, werewolves in their wolf form, and even a harpy with her wings fully extended while she soaked up the sun. But most people looked like me—human.

Paranormals had learned over the centuries to keep their powers and their less-than-human body parts to themselves. Groups had already begun to form as returning students found their old friends.

I walked past a girl sitting under a tree, utterly absorbed in a book. She didn't even look up as a werewolf leaped over her head to catch a frisbee. A pang of wistfulness twisted my stomach. Maybe one day I'd be that comfortable here, losing myself in some Marine Mythology project.

On the far side of the lawn, I spotted three buildings. I scanned the map Headmistress Losia had given me. The biggest building was the dormitory, while the smaller two held classes.

There was a saltwater lake for the mermaids and the Mythical Marine Creatures class, but I would be avoiding that as much as possible. The headmistress had given me special directions to a freshwater pond that was part of her personal property and had given me permission to swim in it as often as I needed.

Freshwater didn't feel as nice as salt water, but I'd need to stretch my tentacles periodically, and I couldn't risk swimming in the public lake.

There was a wooded area on the other side of the lake. When researching Slaymore, I learned it was full of brownies, pixies, and small paranormal creatures that could be studied in the forest mythology class. Sadly, I doubted I'd be spending much time there since I was a creature of the Deep.

Several students had begun watching me, and I was starting to feel weird about hauling my suitcase around. Nothing screamed *new girl* like a suitcase and a wondering expression.

I was delaying because I really didn't want to meet my

roommate. I'd never considered that I might have to share my space. Maybe if I appealed—

*No nonsense,* I told myself sternly.

I was representing the Bering clan and the whole Kraken race. How embarrassing would it be if Krakens got a reputation for being whiny when things didn't go their way?

I'd just have to muscle through a semester at Slaymore with a roomie. Surely, after the first semester, some students would be dropping out, graduating early, or moving in with their boyfriends. Then I could finagle a place of my own.

For now, I'd have to be okay with a roommate.

*I could totally do this.*

As long as she wasn't a hero or a slayer.

Readjusting my grip on the suitcase handle, I straightened my back and made my way to my room.

I unlocked the door to my room with my keycard and found my new roomie standing directly on the other side.

"Rooommie!" she shrieked and threw her arms around me.

It happened so fast I hadn't even had a chance to think about self-defense.

"I'm Ayla, and I'm a succubus." She had a pale, heart-shaped face, shockingly green eyes, and dark pink hair that hung straight and perfect against her killer cheekbones. "But I don't do sex. Promise." Ayla held up a pinky.

I stared at it. She'd painted her nails heart-red and dotted each one with a rhinestone. "Uh, okay."

She looked at me.

I looked at her.

Was I supposed to do something?

Eventually, she dropped her pinky. "Anyway, I'm so excited to be here! And to be with my roomie! I've already got the week planned out! Stick with me, and by Saturday, you'll know exactly where the sickest parties are, who's got the best snacks, and which teachers have the easiest classes."

Without waiting for me to introduce myself, Ayla made her way to her bed, and I finally got a good look at my room.

It was gray. We had a single bed each, with gray sheets and a gray comforter. There was a gray desk at the head of our beds and a gray wardrobe at the foot.

Through the open doorway, I caught a glimpse of the bathroom. It was nice enough. The sink, toilet, and shower were all gray, of course.

Sighing, I opened my suitcase and filled my wardrobe before sticking the empty suitcase beneath my bed.

Ayla's side of the room looked like she'd already been living there for months. Clothes lay everywhere... except in her wardrobe. A bag of chips was open on her desk, and a sketchbook lay on her pillow. The page had a few soft pencil lines on it, so she must have just started drawing as I'd come in.

Stepping over to the window, I stared out at the expansive lawn. It was beautiful, but I found myself wishing I had a view of water instead. I'd been on land less than a day, and it was already starting to feel restrictive.

Plus, my tentacles itched.

"So I already talked to the left side of the hall. We've got a vampire, a witch, two shapeshifters and a banshee in residence... and me." Ayla twirled a pencil between her fingers. "And you. What are you?"

"Isn't that kind of a personal question?" I tried to deflect.

"Yeah. Sorry about that." Ayla groaned. "I'm always talking first and thinking later. You can tell me in your own time. I'm cool with everybody, you know? We're all just people. Looking for fun, love, and life experiences."

"Uh-huh." Was it a succubus's special power to talk someone to death?

I thought succubuses made people horny. Maybe this one tried talking people up to arousal? If so, I could understand why she'd said *no sex*. She sucked at it.

Ayla kept going, oblivious to my inner discussion. "And Tricia's already got guy problems; they broke up, but they're both coming here, so she asked me if I had any anti-love powers—which would be cool—but I don't. Then she said that if I couldn't do *that*, the least I could do was get her a really good one-night stand, which, I'm not really into that side of succubus culture, you know?"

Did she ever stop to breathe? I wasn't sure how long land dwellers could go without air, but Ayla seemed like she'd have great breath control.

I ran my finger along my cuff and looked around my side of the room. It was boring, but I didn't need anything else.

Actually, I did need one more thing. Textbooks.

"I'm going to the bookstore," I said.

Ayla broke off her one-sided conversation and sat up. "Perfect! I'll go with you. Give me a minute."

"You don't have to—"

Ignoring me, Ayla hopped into the bathroom and reappeared a moment later with her hairbrush. "Your hair's lush, by the way. Is the color natural? Sorry, probably another rude question. But if you dye, that ombre is perfection. I'm just saying."

"It's natural," I murmured, not knowing what else to say.

Ayla seemed like an unstoppable force of sociability. And I... I just wanted to be left alone.

"You should *always* tell me if I'm being inappropriate about physical appearance. It's such a big part of succubus culture, and I want to unlearn it, but we literally *exist* to enhance the beauty of things. Have you ever tried to unlearn your entire bloodline? It's insane. My brothers can't believe I'm doing it. Of course, they spend all their time thinking with their— Oh, hang on."

Her phone began ringing. Thank Poseidon and all the gods of the sea!

She answered it and headed back into the bathroom.

Alone, I sat back down on my bed, feeling lost. It felt rude not to wait for her, but I hadn't exactly invited her along either.

Ayla stuck her head out of the bathroom. "Freshman orientation. Five minutes. Should we go and buy books after?"

"I'll just stay in," I decided.

"No orientation?" Her perfect eyes grew wide. "How are you supposed to know where the best coffee shop is? No, wait. I'll tell you. Don't worry. I'll get all the gossip and fill you in. Just don't spend all day moping in here being homesick, okay?"

She brought the phone back up to her ear. "Hey, Kit-Kat. She says she doesn't want to come, but I'm all in."

I ignored Ayla's chatter as she reapplied her mascara and halfheartedly lifted my hand when she waved goodbye at the door. Even after she closed it, I could hear her voice echoing down the hall.

Finally alone, I bounced a bit on the bed, testing it. I'd have to get used to sleeping this way. In the Deep, we mostly floated, but Slaymore had a strict policy about us holding to our human forms at least 90 percent of the time.

It minimized magical incidents, and if a random human somehow got past the wards and onto Slaymore's grounds, it also lowered the chances of them finding out everything.

Online rumors said Headmistress Losia hadn't been seen in her dragon form for decades.

I, of course, would be human pretty much permanently while here.

*And it's what you wanted,* I reminded myself as a wave of homesickness crested inside me.

Slaymore's professor of Marine Mythology was the foremost expert on the topic, and learning from him would be a rare opportunity.

Using this time to prove to other paranormals that

Krakens could keep up with the times and do everything land dwellers could do would be a real boon to our people. I'd be making a difference, forging a path toward our acceptance on land.

Just like Headmistress Losia had done for her people.

Pulling my headphones from the desk drawer, I plugged them into the phone I'd bought when I'd first arrived on land. Tapping through my playlist, I found an album of whale songs. I turned it up, lay back on the bed, and closed my eyes.

Tomorrow, the studying began, and my 'college' experience would continue. But for the rest of today, I just wanted to miss my watery home in peace.

# CHAPTER 3
## SETA

Brilliant sunlight pierced the thin dorm room curtain before six the next morning, startling me awake. As someone used to the gentle awakening of light diffusing through water, I spent my entire shower cursing land and listing all the reasons Slaymore should've been an underwater academy.

Ayla was still asleep when I finished dressing, so I took the opportunity to find a dining hall and get myself some breakfast.

Slaymore's dining halls were divided by cuisine, and it didn't take me long to find the one that catered to mermaids, kelpies, and other water-dwelling paranormals. I loaded a briny-smelling plate with seaweed, fish eggs, and cold smoked salmon.

Once seated, I pulled up the class schedule in my emails

and perused it as I ate. I had a five-class course load, each with three lecture classes and three study hours per week.

In addition to my Marine Mythology class, I'd be studying Beginner's Incantations, Summoning Magic, and Alchemy. I was also required to take an academic writing course as a core class.

The truth was, I was looking forward to everything except academic writing and alchemy. I'd never been good with alchemical substances and had struggled with those during my high school years. Somehow, no matter how carefully I followed the directions, my projects always blew up in my face.

"Look who it is!" A familiar wave of comfort washed through me as Amadeus slid into the chair across from mine.

He was grinning far too widely for someone in a dining hall before seven. "So, have you found everything okay?"

Turning my phone, I showed him my schedule.

"Nice! Alchemy, I've got that too. I also have academic writing—but I'm in a different period. We could do our homework together, though."

My heart wanted to say yes, but my brain knew I needed to stay focused on my goals and not become distracted.

"No, thanks." I slipped my phone back into my pocket.

"*Wow*." Another student set a plate on the table and slid into the chair beside me.

The new guy pushed his dark brown hair out of his eyes. He had a sharp nose and chin and eyes that seemed to dart around the room constantly, as though he were on the lookout. I leaned away from him instinctively.

"That was a serious put-down. I don't think I've ever seen someone shut Deus down like that." He laughed.

It wasn't an easygoing laugh like Amadeus had. Nope. He was definitely laughing at the expense of his friend.

"I just want to get my work done quickly so I can get to bed early each night. Socializing isn't big on my to-do list," I said, hoping it was enough of an excuse. Eyes narrowed, I studied the two men. "What are you even doing in here? You're not sea creatures, either of you."

Had Amadeus been following me? Looking for me?

"Ezric has a mermaid ladyfriend he wants to impress," said Amadeus, not bothering to hide his smirk.

Ezric's smile soured. "I guess when she said she was an early riser, she didn't mean *this* early."

My stomach clenched as I watched Ezric pick up a calamari ring from his plate and pop it in his mouth. I loved fresh seafood but couldn't bring myself to eat calamari... it was just too close to cannibalism.

My face must have shown my queasiness, because Ezric smirked and picked up a second fried ring. "What? You don't like calamari?"

"Um. Not really," I managed to squeak.

Ezric tossed the ring into the air and caught it in his mouth. After chewing, he spoke again. "It's my favorite seafood. Probably because I grew up listening to my dad refer to Kraken meat as the sweetest delicacy of the sea, and this is as close as I can get to tasting it."

My throat had tightened to the point it was strangling me. I wanted to scream or run, but I was frozen in place.

"I can't believe your dad used to participate in those hunts. It's weird that the paranormal council allowed a paranormal species to be hunted." Amadeus snagged a piece of sushi from my plate, his face an unreadable mask.

Did he approve of Krakens being slaughtered? It didn't seem like he did, but I couldn't be sure and couldn't have asked if I'd wanted to.

"Are you kidding? My dad led several of those hunts!" Ezric's chest puffed with pride, and I fought the urge to vomit.

It was hard enough to hear about the cruel murders of my species, but hearing someone gloat about those horrific deaths shocked me to my core. How could I change the opinions of people who didn't even see Krakens as worthy of life?

To my immense relief, Ezric pushed back from the table and stood. "I'm going to go see if I can find my missing mermaid. See you around, Red."

It took me a moment to realize he was talking about the red in my hair. I looked at Amadeus, expecting him to stand and follow his friend.

I found, for the first time since arriving at Slaymore, I didn't want to be alone.

My heart longed for Amadeus to stay.

He shrugged, giving me a smile that eased some of the anxiety that had welled up inside me at Ezric's words. "I'm up for anything. How's the salmon?"

## KRAMMIN' WITH A KRAKEN

It seemed like everyone at Slaymore was determined to be as friendly as possible. Although, I couldn't help but wonder how many of them would join Ezric and his father in a Kraken hunt if given a chance.

Amadeus stuck around for breakfast, then walked with me to get textbooks since I'd fallen asleep early the night before. With the muscular hunk at my side, a sense of calm settled over me.

I felt safe at his side, which could spell disaster for me if I let myself become involved with him... because how safe could I be when Amadeus's closest friend enjoyed hunting my kind?

I took my time in the store, enjoying the experience of being surrounded by books. When I stumbled upon the novel section, I realized how hungry I was for a good book.

Kraken libraries were precious things, difficult to protect from the water and often filled with whatever books we salvaged from the ocean floor. So, being in a store filled from floor-to-ceiling with mint-condition books was a treat.

I jumped, clutching my chest, when someone tapped me on the shoulder. I'd completely lost myself in a fantasy about mermaid politics and hadn't even noticed that Amadeus had disappeared.

Twisting around in my chair, I found myself face-to-face

with the store clerk. "Are you buying those books? Because class starts in five minutes—"

"I need to go!" I shot out of the seat.

There was no way I could be late for my first class. They'd never let me take independent study if I started off with a record like that.

Quickly buying the textbooks—and the fantasy novel—I sprinted outside. Pulling out my map, I searched for the location of my academic writing class.

Academic Writing was held in one of the smaller buildings off the lawn. It was a one-story half-circle structure with yet another fountain in front of it.

The statue in the middle of the fountain was decorated with a fey... a *real* fey. The kind with wings, claws, and razor-sharp teeth that could rip your arm off.

The sculptor had captured her unearthly beauty in bronze, and she gave off an alluring quality—like she'd rip my arm off, and I'd like it.

Jogging across the dew-covered grass, I was one of the last to arrive in the class and slipped into the last empty chair near the front. The class was unusually quiet. Since this was a first-year requirement class, perhaps no one had had a chance to make friends yet.

Our writing teacher seemed nice enough, but she didn't teach me anything I didn't already know. I took notes for the sake of it, though, and was careful to keep my head down.

At the end of the class, I went up to her with my notebook prominently displayed. "Miss Halyet? I mean, Professor?"

Professor Halyet had bronze skin and a tail that flicked back and forth behind her. It was the only thing that indicated what kind of paranormal she was. She nodded graciously to me, causing her brown curls to bounce.

"So, I've done a lot of academic writing," I began.

"And you want to skip my class?" she guessed in her husky voice, making me think she must get this all the time.

"No!" Well, that would be ideal, but I knew I wouldn't get away with it. "I just... I do my best studying on my own. It's what I'm used to, and I think I could really give you my best work through independent study."

She sorted through the stacks of papers on her desk. "I'm afraid that's not possible."

"I'll turn in everything. You could even give me more complicated assignments," I pushed, not ready to give up. "Here! I'll email you a paper I wrote, and you can see for yourself—"

"I know you're a good student, Seta," Professor Halyet interrupted, her voice gentle. "But part of the Slaymore experience is learning to work with others. The paranormal experience often leaves us suspicious of outsiders. Believe it or not, sitting in class with your peers will help you with that."

I didn't believe it, and I opened my mouth to say so, but Professor Halyet fixed me with a prim look that made me shut it again.

It was clear I wouldn't get anywhere with her, so I

nodded. Hoping I didn't look too disappointed, I turned and headed for my next class.

*You only need one yes,* I tried to reassure myself. *Word will get around about how studious you are, and then all the professors will let you do what you like.*

"No." Professor Mackenzie, my Marine Mythology professor, was firm.

My shoulders slumped.

It was Friday, and my last lecture of the week started in five minutes. None of my teachers had agreed to let me study independently, and I no longer had the energy to plead my case.

It was time for Plan B.

If I had to prove myself, I would prove myself. I'd already spent my first two study periods flicking through the textbook, so I knew I could get the job done in Marine Mythology.

Thanking the professor, I scurried back to my seat and took out my laptop.

"Deus!" someone called, and my eyes moved to the door as though a string were pulling me.

Amadeus shared this class with me, and I low-key hated it.

I disliked the tumultuous emotions inside me that made

me want to run to his side and give him a hug. And I hated the way his smile made me bite my lip.

At least I knew my reactions were magically inspired. Almost every female on campus looked at Amadeus as though he held the answer to all their prayers.

It wasn't just the girls who were affected by him. Guys were eager to banter with him and offer countless invites to their parties. Amadeus was magnetic somehow.

I hadn't figured out his species yet, but maybe he was an incubus?

Deus gave out several high-fives and nodded to a girl in the front row, who stretched like a circus performer, unabashedly showing off her arching back and lifting breasts.

I rolled my eyes and looked down at my laptop.

"Let's get started." Professor Mackenzie clapped his hands, and Deus took a seat in the back with a muttered apology.

I leaned forward, focusing on the professor. Not only did I want to ace this class, but Mackenzie had a Scottish burr that I could barely understand.

For the next hour, my fingers flew over my keyboard as I tried to write everything he said, word for word. Mackenzie was a genius.

He'd confirmed the existence of the Loch Ness monster. After that, he'd spearheaded a thirty-man team that had transported her from her loch and into private waters where she wouldn't be discovered or harassed by humans.

Professor Mackenzie had studied a dozen different

mermaid communes, discovered several previously unknown shifter forms, and even opened communication with the Skopuna Kraken clan.

He'd been quoted in articles as saying that for every shifter form he'd met in the sea, there must have been hundreds more that remained a mystery.

And after earning my degrees, I planned to make it my life's work to find them all.

At the end of the lecture, he paused to take a long drink of water. Setting the bottle down, he leaned back against his desk and addressed us again.

"You'll remember your syllabus has a paired project. An in-depth study of the marine myth of your choice. Each group needs to pick a different myth, so the sooner you agree and come to me, the better. I've paired you up already. Settle down!"

The outbreak of chatter that had accompanied his announcement quieted instantly.

"I'm only going to read the list once. If you're not listening, tough on you." He rattled off names, waiting until each student raised their hand.

My name was fifth on the list.

"Seta sa Bering"—his eyes found mine—"Amadeus Koidos."

Behind me, I heard more than one wistful sigh, but it took all my willpower to keep my head from dropping against the desk.

The more time I spent with Amadeus, the more certain I

became that I was playing with a dangerous hurricane that could wreck my life and the lives of my clan.

Ayla had already warned me how much group work sucked, but I'd rather do the whole project with a partner who sat on his phone than try to wrangle work out of a party-life-loving partner I was drawn to like a moth to a flame.

Maybe Mackenzie would let me switch? After all, there were loads of people who'd love to be partnered with shining Deus and his dazzling smile.

"What are the odds?" Amadeus made his way to my side as soon as the bell rang. "High-five, new partner!"

He held up his hand, and I halfheartedly patted my hand against his. "Anyway, I'm due for a round of frisbee golf. If you want to tag along, we can discuss what myth we want to work on."

I'd already thought about the project. "Narwhal shifters."

It was one of the shifter forms Mackenzie had discovered, but even he admitted they were a secretive bunch. Acing this project would prove to him that I was serious about my studies.

Amadeus's smile didn't dim, but something flickered through his eyes. "What's a narwhal?"

Huffing, I ran a hand through my hair. "You don't know what a narwhal is? Why are you even taking Marine Mythology?"

Deus gave me a sheepish smile. "To learn what a narwhal is. Among other things. Anyway, I trust you. If you say narwhal shifters, then narwhal shifters it is! Brief me on what you know as we walk, and we'll make a game plan."

"I'm not going to frisbee golf." I shoved my laptop into my bag, cringing at how rude I probably sounded.

Amadeus was undeterred. "Okay. So where are you headed now?"

My stomach chose that moment to rumble. "The dining hall," I admitted.

Having been too wrapped up in the frustrating alchemy forms to remember the time, I'd managed to miss lunch.

"Cool. The dining hall's on the way. We'll go together." He shifted his backpack to the other shoulder.

My stomach did a weird little flip-flop despite me telling it to calm down because there was no reason to be excited about spending more time with him.

But we *did* have to talk about our project. Even if it was only to establish that I'd do the work and he could just leave me alone. I shouldered my own bag and followed him out onto the lawn.

The whole week had been full of sun, but heavy, dark clouds had gathered on the horizon over the course of the early afternoon. A thunderstorm was supposed to break tonight, and I fully planned to use the bad weather to sneak off to Headmistress Losia's freshwater pond for a much-needed swim.

I stumbled when Deus came to an unexpected stop. He drew in a deep breath. The glow that clung to him seemed to pulse, and his full lips parted.

My eyes followed the sleek line of his throat down to the

little triangle of skin that peeked out from under his button-up shirt.

He caught me looking. "The smell of rain. There's nothing like it."

I looked up at the clouds so he couldn't see me blush. "I, uh… didn't take you for a rain spirit."

"I'm not. I'm a lightning bolt. We're related but not the same." Gesturing for me to follow, he set off toward the dining hall.

"A living lightning bolt? I've never heard of a species like that." There was so much about the species who lived on land and in the skies that I didn't know.

Deus nodded. He didn't seem offended—then again, he didn't seem like anything would offend him.

"I've got six brothers, and we're it. The only lightning bolts in the world." He chuckled and added, "Unless my dad decides to make more."

"Your dad?" I arched an eyebrow. "Don't you need a mom for that, too?"

"Nope." Deus flicked a finger, and a little *zap* of electricity shot into the air, forming a miniature lightning bolt.

Two clouds formed and clapped together a moment later, releasing a thunder boom no louder than a cough. "You got born, we got made. By the Greek god himself."

Deus was the son of a god.

"Zeus, right?" I hadn't had many dealings with Zeus since Poseidon was the main Greek god Krakens dealt with.

"Yep."

"That's… neat." I didn't want to admit how curious I

was, and I bit my tongue to keep my countless questions from tumbling out.

Deus lifted one shoulder. "It's all right. I have a few cool powers, and I have some not-so-cool powers. Although, I guess that's true for everyone."

We walked for several feet before he spoke again.

"I'm really glad to be paired with you." He grinned at me again, and a ridiculous flutter began in my chest. "I'm 100 percent completely and totally terrified of the sea, so I couldn't ask for a better partner than a mermaid. You're a mermaid, right?"

I hesitated, finding it harder than I expected to lie to Deus.

"Right..." It was what Headmistress Losia and I had agreed I would claim. But the lie tasted like acrid ash on my tongue.

Because I wasn't a mermaid, and I didn't want to *be* a mermaid.

I was here to change perspectives, I reminded myself. Get people to see I wasn't a threat... that I was a person, too. Then maybe the next time a Kraken came to Slaymore, they wouldn't have to hide.

But how long would I have to keep my secret before I could reveal my species without risking life and tentacle?

Deus was studying me a little too closely, a strange expression on his face. I needed to change the subject.

"You're terrified of the sea?" I asked. "Why are you taking Marine Mythology if you're terrified of the sea?"

"I need to get three biome credits. And I like to face my fears."

Facing his fears. It was the sensible thing to do. You ruled your fear, not the other way around.

Still... "How could you be afraid of the water? You're lightning and could probably kill half the life in the lake."

Deus ran a hand through his blonde hair. "Well, yeah. But I'd hurt myself and everything around me. If that's not something to be afraid of, I don't know what is."

We'd crossed the full length of the lawn and stood in front of the dining hall. Someone ran by us, calling to Amadeus and holding up a frisbee.

"Be right there!" Deus shouted back. Then he turned to me. "So, narwhal shifters? I'll check out the library after frisbee golf. Any good tips on where I should start?"

"Just leave it to me." I clutched the strap of my backpack. "I'll tell you what to say in the presentation. Don't worry, you'll look good."

Deus's smile turned quizzical, and he cocked his head. "Are you sure you know how group projects work?"

Leaning forward, he put a hand on my arm. Warmth shot through my arm, running straight to my belly, and my heart stumbled over its beat.

"We'll talk about it later. Don't worry. I don't know much about narwhals, but I'll learn."

I could barely register what he said as goosebumps rippled across my body.

When he finally moved his hand, the place where his

fingers had touched my skin was still warm. He gave me a playful wink and turned to follow his friend.

Watching Deus jog away, my eyes roved over his body, ignoring my brain's demands that I look away.

I couldn't help but appreciate the way his shoulders moved under his shirt, nor could I stop my eyes from traveling down his spine to where his tight-fitting chinos showed off his—

*Stop this nonsense,* I chided myself. Crossing my arms, I turned toward the dining hall door.

Oh, how my mother would *love* for my first message home to be filled with guy talk. *If* I did anything—and I wouldn't—it would be purely physical. Maybe a bit of fun to relieve the stress of my studies and the pressure I was under.

I wasn't so stupid that I'd get involved with a guy who could tank my project and possibly my goals, if things went wrong.

# CHAPTER 4
## SETA

The storm broke during dinner, sending cascading sheets of water down to earth, where it turned the gravel paths that traversed the campus to mud.

The crowded marine dining hall watched in amusement as the landlocked paranormals ran under the cover of umbrellas, coats, backpacks… and under the wings of a generous vampire who'd shifted into a huge bat.

I listened to—a.k.a. eavesdropped on—the conversation happening between a selkie, a mermaid, and a siren as they excitedly debated everything from their thesis projects to their favorite cheesecake-ice cream combination.

A small part of me wished to have friends I could laugh with and tease, but I firmly pushed that piece of myself to a dark corner of my mind. I was here to get my degrees, prove that Krakens weren't monsters, and then get back to the sea as soon as possible.

Around nine, I wrapped my raincoat around my backpack and eagerly set off for the freshwater pond. Passing the lake, I could hear mermaids splashing as they took turns diving for stones. My sensitive hearing allowed me to pick up their singing as they swam beneath the water's surface.

I winced at the sharp pang of longing that stabbed my chest, and my tentacles strained against their enchantment. I shouldn't have to slink around, but I reminded myself of the necessity.

Until we could prove that I was no threat, I had to keep my secret to protect my clan and my kind.

"Suck it up, buttercup. Or maybe it should be suction-cup?" I mumbled.

Headmistress Losia's house and grounds lay on the far side of the fae wood. I skirted the forest, walking in the open rain until I came to a small brick house.

It was a sturdy building with a tin roof and surrounded by a wrought-iron fence. The front gate was locked but low enough that I could easily step over it.

Glancing toward the house, I spotted Headmistress Losia standing at the window and waved. She gave me a bright smile and lifted her hand in greeting.

Rain pattered through the leaves, plastering my ombre hair to my head and causing my clothes to suction against my skin. *Next time I should bring a hat.* My hair was too distinctive, and the last thing I needed was for someone to follow me.

I followed an ancient flagstone path into a small cluster of trees and finally found the pond. It was set into the stone, dotted with water lilies, and populated by a few lazy koi.

Tucking my bag under a stone bench, I shed my clothes and let the rain tickle my bare skin. I breathed deeply, filling my lungs with the humid evening air.

Deus was right. The smell of rain was something truly beautiful.

Sitting down on the edge of an overhanging rock, I slid in. The pond was deeper than I'd expected. It was deep enough to dive, and the cool water was like a balm on skin that had been dry and overly warm all week.

Taking a last furtive glance around, I made sure no one was watching. Seeing no one, I held my breath and slipped the gold cuff off my wrist.

I was too large in my fully shifted, eight-tentacled Kraken form to fit in the pond, so I'd chosen to perform a partial shift. My legs transformed into tentacles as red as my hair, and four more tentacles sprouted to join them.

From the waist up, I appeared similar to a mermaid. Faint scales glowed against my skin, and gills had formed thin lines on either side of my neck.

The only way I differed from a mer was my darkened fingertips, which looked as though they'd been dipped in black ink, and the swirling imprint lines that wrapped my wrists and forearms. Another Kraken would recognize the importance of those lines, but they would be completely invisible to anyone outside my species.

Since Krakens were typically killed in their fully shifted beast form, it wasn't likely that anyone would recognize my species even if they did catch sight of my darkened hands and fingers.

A Kraken's eight tentacles were similar to those of an octopus or cuttlefish, but the tips had a feathery fin on them, perfect for doing nearly anything fingers could do.

The curious koi circled around me, and I ran the tip of one tentacle along their backs. Then, I submerged completely.

Beneath the water, I could speak to them in my own language. That way, they were more likely to understand. For several minutes, I played with the koi, pushing the currents of the pond gently this way and that.

When they drifted away to find a snack, I stretched my tentacles. Using them to search out the depth of the pond, I found a rock at the bottom that would be good for scrubbing.

Taking my time, I used the stone as an abrasive against my skin. The scrubbing left me feeling tingly and wide awake. I looked up toward the water's surface at the wavering image of the treetops and the deep night beyond.

All in all, my first week at Slaymore had been good. I'd caused no ambassadorial incidents, I'd gotten a good start to all my classes, and I'd taken stock of the academy's glorious library. Most importantly, I'd kept my secret.

And despite my roommate's best attempts, I'd even

managed to keep to myself. Ayla was all right, but I'd been relieved once I'd learned that when I put in my headphones, she'd leave me alone.

She was really *nice*. In fact, other than Ezric, I hadn't met anyone mean at Slaymore yet.

Though, I might've preferred it if Amadeus was a jerk… or at least uninteresting. It would have made it easier to ignore the invisible thread that seemed to be pulling me toward him.

It just wasn't fair that he emitted that golden aura, or had the bluest of blue eyes, or fingers I could still feel hours later…

Not to mention, his body wasn't bad, either. Those full lips had probably kissed their fair share of girls. He certainly had plenty of opportunities.

My body warmed as I imagined how it might feel to kiss a mouth like that.

It wasn't like I was completely inexperienced. I'd kissed a few harpies—something I definitely didn't recommend.

Sadly, I'd never scored a flirt with a merman.

Kissing a Kraken was a no-go as well. I was related to everyone in the Bering clan, and Kraken clans didn't mingle often. When they did, it was only for well-meaning parents to force a mate upon their offspring in a desperate effort to preserve our kind.

I wanted a toe-curling kiss, not to be bound for life to someone I didn't know.

Regardless, sea creatures didn't have a reputation for warm mouths.

But Deus...

Just thinking his name had my tentacles curling.

I bet Deus looked delectable with his shirt off. Closing my eyes, I imagined him standing outside the pond, undoing each mother-of-pearl button on his shirt and flexing his shoulders as he bared his skin to the night sky.

He'd take off his trousers next, revealing muscled thighs and calves as golden as his chest. And then he'd hook his thumbs in the band of his boxers and slid—

A rippling current bubbled up to the surface of the pond, sending a crest of water rushing over the stones. I winced, knowing I'd probably just soaked my backpack.

Embarrassment flooded my body, and I opened my eyes. Was I really fantasizing about some landlocked guy after spending only a few hours in his company?

I needed to be focused on my future, not daydreaming about Deus. Sure, my mother and the rest of the clan would be delighted for me to be mated to a land-dweller, but I'd refused to allow them to force me to become a mate. I wanted to learn, experience adventures, and help make the seas and land safer for Krakens.

I longed to be something more.

The water around me grew heated with my agitation, causing the koi to dart to the far edges of the pond.

Closing my eyes, I tightened an imaginary fist around my emotions. Making the water even half a degree warmer could destroy the delicate balance of life in the pond.

That wasn't what a Kraken did.

We were keepers of the balance.

I had to control myself. Opening my gills, I breathed deeply, focusing on the ebb and flow of the surrounding water.

The freshwater tasted odd in comparison to the salty waters of my home, but it was still comforting after breathing air for the past week.

When I was sure I was in control again, I opened my eyes.

Fantasizing about a classmate shouldn't be a problem. Everyone had to blow off steam sometimes... even me.

As long as I could keep the fantasy under control, it might even help. A tentacle with a mind of its own began to slide around my hips. I could take care of my personal needs in private, and no one—especially Deus—would be the wiser.

No difficult entanglements, no friends with benefits who wanted something more. It wouldn't be as satisfying as touching Deus's skin and feeling his lips against mine, but it would be the safest option.

Glancing up, I watched as lightning sizzled across the dark sky and reflected on the rippling surface of the water. Night had fallen, and it would provide me the cover I needed.

I swam up, and breaking the surface, I rested my arms on the cold stones surrounding the pond. In this position, I could release most of my energy into the air instead of directly into the water, which would hopefully help me avoid boiling the koi if I lost control again.

Closing my eyes, I pressed my forehead against my

folded arms and allowed my earlier fantasy to drift back into my mind...

*Deus walked to stand by the edge of the pond, his eyes swirling with the promise of things to come. His long fingers slowly undid each button on his shirt, leaving a trail of flashing lights from his fingertips.*

*What would those flashes of electricity feel like against my skin? Deus kneeled in front of me, not caring that he was soaking his pants. Reaching out, his fingers trailed up my bare arm and down my exposed ribs.*

*I bit my lip to keep from moaning.*

*"Let me join you, gorgeous." Deus's voice was a low rumble that had my stomach and other parts clenching with need. "Let me touch you."*

*He paused, waiting for my agreement. I'd spent too much time ignoring my body's needs, and the demands for release were reaching a fever pitch. At my nod of agreement, Deus kicked off his shoes and slid into the water beside me.*

*My muscles trembled as I fought the urge to wrap my tentacles around him and take what I wanted from him. Lowering myself into the water, I held my breath as Deus moved behind me.*

*Keeping one hand on the edge of the water, he used his body to pin me against the bank of the pond. His erection pressed into the curve of my butt, showing me the effect I had on him.*

*One of my tentacles moved to curl around his waist, pulling him tighter against me and helping to keep him afloat. Deus didn't recoil; instead, his fingers teased across the sensitive suction cups, causing me to whimper and arch against him.*

*I was an adult Kraken, which meant having my tentacles*

*touched in my partially shifted form was as erotic as having him stroke my clit. It was the first time anyone had touched my tentacles, and I nearly came apart.*

*"Please. I need your touch." I didn't care that I was begging.*

*Deus chuckled. Moving his hand up my stomach, he cupped my breast and squeezed gently as his thumb teased the hardened peak of my nipple. With my tentacles supporting him, Deus let go of the bank and dropped his hand beneath the water.*

*When his fingers moved across my hip to brush against the aching slit between my tentacles, a torrent of lust exploded through every cell in my body, robbing me of breath.*

*"Tell me what you need," Deus said between kisses as his lips moved along my neck.*

*"I need you," I panted.*

*Deus responded by slipping two fingers inside my heat. I was almost sobbing as his fingers stretched me, and when he brushed against my G-spot, I had to clench my fingers on the stones to keep from drowning.*

*Never had I imagined the pleasure of being touched by a man would be this mind-blowing. No, not just any man. I didn't understand it, but there was a part of me that knew only intimacy with Deus would be this incredible.*

*As his fingers found their rhythm, I rocked against his palm. My pleasure was building to a crescendo, and I knew I wasn't going to last more than a couple seconds.*

*"Please, Deus," I pleaded, desperate for release.*

"Tell me how I can help you."

It took my brain several seconds to realize the voice hadn't been inside my head.

Opening my eyes, I blinked hard, my eyes trying to focus on the kneeling form of Deus in front of me.

A very real Deus.

Lightning flashed around him, and in his pupils as he studied me. How much had he heard? Or seen?

Those questions and his presence should have been enough to fully tear me away from the fantasy, but my mind was still stuck between what was real and what I had imagined... and my body was too close to my release for me to stop the tidal wave of pleasure bearing down on me.

My tentacles had a mind of their own, and the one pretending to be Deus's fingers between my legs continued to stroke me. I trembled violently, biting my lip to keep from moaning. Reaching out his left hand, Deus wrapped his warm palm around my arm, steadying me.

I needed to stop before he figured out what was going on beneath the water. If he realized I was pleasuring myself with him right in front of me, he'd probably think I was a complete freak.

"You said you needed me. What do you need? Are you hurt?" Deus brushed his fingers across my cheek, and a shock like static electricity sizzled through me.

This time, his touch on my skin was real, not something I imagined, and it was my undoing.

"Deus." My voice cracked, and I fought to keep my body from convulsing as I climaxed harder than I'd ever experienced while handling my personal needs.

If sexy times with Amadeus were this incredible in my mind, I couldn't imagine how I would survive the real thing. It was probably for the best that I would never find out.

But as Deus's fingers brushed my hair from my face, I found myself second-guessing that decision.

"Seta?" Deus's voice slowly came back into focus.

It took a couple of tries, but I managed to croak, "I'm fine. I'm not hurt."

"You're shaking." Cupping my jaw, Deus lifted my face so he could search my eyes.

I shivered at his touch even as the aftershocks of pleasure were rippling through me. "The water is a little cold, that's all."

Deus's nostrils flared, and miniature lightning streaked across his skin. "Are you sure?"

"Yes. I'm definitely fine." Needing to change the subject, I narrowed my eyes. "Why are you here?"

Deus's eyes darted away from me, and he shrugged. "The storm picked up, and I was worried you may have gotten lost. I came to check the woods and heard my name."

*Great Poseidon!*

I hadn't meant to say his name out loud! How much more had I said aloud?

Deus was still talking, and swallowing back my rising panic, I tried to focus.

"Anyway, I followed your voice and found you here in the pool. You appeared to be in pain, and I thought you'd been injured. I didn't mean to intrude." His eyes dropped to my hands, and his finger tapped one of my imprint lines.

"These are beautiful, Seta."

I flushed with pleasure at his words, causing my scales to flicker and glow.

Then logic kicked in.

"Wh-what are you talking about?" How had he been able to see the imprints? Something unfamiliar unfurled in my chest.

*Mine.*

Mine? That was weird. He was my project partner, and that was it.

"Your tattoos. The artist is insanely talented." His finger traced one of the lines, and I was shocked when my body responded as though he were touching me in a far more intimate place.

"Thank you." I quivered, still more than a little confused about how Deus could see them and why my body was responding so dramatically to him. "I'd rather no one else know I have tattoos. Okay?"

"Of course. I won't tell anyone, but you know they'll see them if they swim with you?" Deus gave me a crooked smile.

I let my body sink a little deeper into the water. "Only if I shift forms, and that's not something I like doing around people."

Deus rubbed his chin. "Really? Most of the mermaids around campus seem to want to stay shifted as much as possible."

"Only because they are hoping to show off their bodies and catch your attention," I mumbled low enough that

Deus would have to be an elephant with a name that rhymes with Morton to hear me.

Amadeus laughed. "That would be a shame."

"Why do you say that?" The words were out before I could swallow them.

"Because they're wasting their time." Deus stood and looked around. "Where's your stuff? Do you want me to put your clothes by the edge so you can change?"

"Um. Yeah?" I bit my lip, trying to figure out how to ask him to leave. My heart was pleading with me to drag him into the water and—

And what?

*Claim him.*

How could I want to claim a man I'd never even kissed? It was proof that I was treading dangerous waters when it came to Amadeus. If I wasn't careful, I'd find myself mated and forced to stay on land.

That wasn't my dream.

No. I wanted to get my degree, prove that Krakens could walk among other species without killing anyone in a murderous rage, and then spend the rest of my life free to explore the seas.

"Here you go. They are a little wet." Amadeus had grabbed my soaked clothing and the gold cuff and placed it in front of me. "I'll go ahead and leave so you can have privacy."

With my form partially shifted, I could easily see in the darkness, and I would swear I caught a faint blush on his cheeks when his eyes trailed over my bare shoulders.

A naughty part of me wanted to rise in the water and watch his expression as more of my skin was exposed, but I quickly tamped down on the urge. I wasn't a siren, so where were these desires to seduce him coming from?

Summoning my willpower, I smiled up at him. "Thank you, Deus. See you tomorrow?"

Deus scratched the back of his neck, and lightning flickered in his eyes before he nodded. "Yeah. Tomorrow."

I watched him until he was out of sight and then listened until his footsteps faded away. When I was sure he was gone, I reached for the cuff.

If I'd been given a choice, I'd have spent the night in the pond, but I didn't want to be forced to explain my soaked walk of shame to Ayla the next morning.

Reluctantly, I slid the gold cuff on, and allowed the shift to ripple over my body. I stayed in the pond until I was sure my body was fully human again.

Pulling on my wet clothes, I grabbed my damp backpack and shoes as I set off down the flagstone path back to Slaymore's official campus grounds.

Unlocking the door to my room, I tiptoed over to the wardrobe. I thought I was doing a dang good job of being sneaky, but as I pulled out my robe, I heard Ayla's sleepy voice.

"Where've you been? Bottom of the lake?"

Her guess was far too close for my comfort.

"Out." I kept my tone flat, hoping it would shut down the conversation. I was still too raw from both my imagined and real encounters with Deus and needed time to process everything.

"Whatever. Put a towel down so I don't slip tomorrow morning, 'kay?" She rolled over.

I crept to the bathroom, and by the time I was finished brushing my teeth and returned to the bedroom, she was breathing the deep, peaceful breaths of sleep.

Tired and relaxed for the first time since coming to land, I crawled into my bed and fell asleep before my head hit the pillow.

# CHAPTER 5
## AMADEUS

I sat at my dorm room desk, staring unseeing out the window.

Seta had looked breathtaking today; although, when did she ever look less than perfect?

*So why haven't you told her?* The words circled around my mind.

I could carry on a conversation with anyone. Professor, student, guys, girls, the homeless guy I bought a coffee for every weekend… but whenever I was in the presence of the flame-haired beauty, my tongue seemed to tie itself in knots.

It wasn't just her beauty that caused the reaction, though. I loved the intelligence that sparkled in her eyes and the stubborn set of her chin when she had made up her mind about something.

I loved the gentleness that radiated from her when she

thought no one was watching, and the adorable shyness that caused her to spin the gold bangle she always wore on her wrist.

Was I falling in love with her?

I couldn't be, could I?

My father told my brothers and me that we weren't capable of falling in love. Living lightning could experience sizzling passion and could even fall in lust… but never love.

Most paranormal species felt the pull of a mate bond, drawing them toward a mate who was a perfect match. But, according to my father, since he hadn't required a female to produce offspring, there was no biological reason for him to have a mate.

If Zeus deemed my brothers and me worthy of producing offspring and blessed us with that ability in the future, we wouldn't need a mate, either. If you didn't need a mate, the mate bond couldn't exist.

But if that were true… then why was I drawn to her every waking minute? How had I been pulled outside by an invisible string on the day she'd arrived? How had I been able to feel her presence inside the car before her driver had even opened the door?

Why did my powers go a little haywire whenever she was near me? Why had I developed a tremor when I hadn't been near her for several hours? A tremor that I fought to hide and only went away after I was near her.

When we were sitting near each other, I could feel her

emotions washing through me as though we were connected, but that was an ability lightnings didn't possess.

My species burned hot, causing our passions and tempers to burn out of control—which made it easier to understand the intense attraction and the overwhelming desire to get her into my bed... and keep her there for a long time. But I didn't just crave sex. If that was all it was, I'd recognize the fiery emotion.

No, I longed for more.

I wanted to touch her hair, to have her rest her head on my shoulder while we read, to hold hands as we walked, to feed her bites of her favorite chocolate, to see her eyes light up with humor as she laughed at my idiocy, and to hold her while I cried over a sappy movie.

Every fiber of my being wanted to wake up with her in my arms every morning for the rest of my life.

All of those things were the textbook signs of a mating pull. So why did I experience them with Seta if the Fates didn't intend for me to have a bonded?

Thunder sounded outside my window, shaking the building. A flash of lightning flickered across the sky. The storm was picking up, and Seta still hadn't returned to her dorm.

What if she was hurt or had gotten lost? She was still new to the campus and might have wandered into the woods without realizing it.

*I should go check on her.*

Shoving to my feet, I hesitated. What if Seta thought I

was acting like an obsessive stalker instead of a concerned friend? She was an adult and could take care of herself.

Except I wanted to take care of her, too.

*Need.*

My heart constricted as the unexpected emotion curled tight fingers around it.

I rubbed my forehead, hoping to clear the confused fog from my mind. This wasn't my need I was experiencing.

Was it from Seta? I hadn't picked up her emotions from a distance before.

*NEED.*

Suddenly sure it was coming from Seta, I hit the floor running, skidding down the hallway and into the darkening evening light.

I didn't even stop to think about where she was, and instead, I allowed the bond to pull me toward her as I leaped over the headmistress's short gate and sprinted down the slick stone path.

The air smelled of petrichor and the wet earth of the forest. Lightning flashed overhead, and I breathed in the heady scent of ozone it left in its wake.

Running through storms was nothing new to me, and in fact, was one of the greatest pleasures in my life. But not tonight. Not with worry for Seta pounding inside my skull and tightening my chest.

Coming to the edge of the clearing, I could just make out a small form in the large pond.

*Seta.*

My steps slowed as I studied the scene in front of me, searching for signs of a threat.

Seta's lower body was submerged, but her arms were clinging to the soaked stones around the pool as though she were trying to keep from slipping beneath the surface of the dark water.

I opened my mouth to speak and alert her to my presence, but Seta spoke first.

"I need you," she gasped in quick, shallow breaths.

Seta must have seen me step into the clearing, although I hadn't seen her eyes open, and she hadn't actually said my name. Was there someone else in the clearing? I quickly scanned the area but found it empty other than for Seta and myself.

"Please, Deus."

My hesitation disappeared the instant my name fell from her lips. Closing the distance between us, I dropped to my knees in front of her. My stomach was clenching with a desperate, driving need that wasn't my own.

"Tell me how I can help you." Fear was tightening its fist around my heart as I searched her face and arms for injuries.

I couldn't find a single mark on her skin that would explain the pained expression twisting her beautiful facial features or cause her rough breathing. Maybe the water was hiding her injuries?

Static popped and flitted across my skin as my worry grew.

*Rein it in, De. If you lose control, you won't be of any use to her,* I reminded myself.

It had been years since my power had tried to push past the barriers I'd built to hold it back. What was it about Seta that seemed to call to my very soul?

Seta's eyes blinked open, and her breath caught.

She was surprised to find me in front of her, which was strange since she'd called for me by name.

The little beauty in front of me was shaking, and something shimmered in the depths of her eyes as she stared up at me. I thought she was going to speak, but she bit her lip instead, trapping an odd gurgling sound in her chest.

Unable to resist the urge to touch her, I wrapped my fingers around her arms, hoping to steady her so she wouldn't slip beneath the surface of the dark water and drown. Could a mermaid drown?

Tiny ripples like the rings around a dropped stone traveled from Seta's body, probably from where she was treading water. Seta remained silent, and her large, luminous eyes were glazed over as though she were somewhere else.

"You said you needed me. What do you need? Are you hurt?" I slid my fingers across Seta's cheek, wincing when my charged-up static popped between our skin.

"Deus," her husky voice cracked, and a certain part of my anatomy stood up and took notice.

My brain was still trying to puzzle out what was going on with the tiny mermaid, but my body recognized the pitch of her voice. It was exactly how I imagined she would say my name as she orgasmed around my cock.

I wanted to pull her from the water and onto my lap so I could show her just how much she affected me. Shaking my head, I tried to clear the lust from my mind. This wasn't the time. I gritted my teeth and prayed Seta wouldn't notice the pitched tent between my legs.

Desperate to touch her, I brushed her hair from her pale face. "Seta?"

Her mouth opened and closed several times before she managed to squeak out, "I'm fine. I'm not hurt."

Gently catching her jaw, I turned her face, still searching for the cause of her strange behavior. "You're shaking."

"The water is a little cold, that's all." Seta shivered again. Her pupils were dilated, her eyelids grew heavy, and her skin glowed.

Then, her scent drifted toward me. I wasn't a werewolf, so I'd never been particularly talented at recognizing smells. But somehow, my body recognized the scent of pleasure. Seta's pleasure.

Who had been here touching her? Satisfying her?

*She was mine.*

I searched the clearing once more, lightning crackling overhead to light the clearing. No one else was here.

And she'd called my name.

A new thought slammed into my already reeling mind.

Maybe Seta was just as attracted to me as I was to her.

Maybe she had been touching herself while thinking of me.

Had she continued teasing herself while I'd been right in front of her? Between that mental image and the delicious scent of her desire filling my lungs, I'd grown painfully hard.

I longed to tell her she could use my body as her personal toy, but I knew it would likely embarrass her if she knew that I knew.

Hope, delight, and raw hunger warred inside me. I might have a chance with her as long as I didn't blow it.

Trying to keep my voice steady, I pretended I was still confused. "Are you sure?"

"Yes. I'm definitely fine." Her eyes grew more focused, and she squinted up at me. "Why are you here?"

I shrugged, trying to breathe through my mouth to keep from drawing in more of her intoxicating scent. "The storm picked up, and I was worried you may have gotten lost. I came to check the woods and heard my name. Anyway, I followed your voice and found you here in the pool. You appeared to be in pain, and I thought you'd been injured. I didn't mean to intrude." Unable to meet her piercing gaze, I looked down, taking in her tattoos for the first time. "These are beautiful, Seta."

Her breath caught, and faint scales glowed a soft orange across her skin. "Wh-what are you talking about?"

As though pulled by a magnet, I slid my fingertip along the swirling lines. "Your tattoos. The artist is insanely talented."

I'd never seen anything like the art, a mix of leaves and flourishes blended with symbols I didn't recognize.

"Thank you." Seta trembled. "I'd rather no one else know I have tattoos. Okay?"

Curiosity had me on the verge of asking her the meaning behind them, but I worried Seta would consider it crossing a line and might not appreciate answering questions.

"Of course. I won't tell anyone, but you know they'll see them if they swim with you?"

She was acting like I was the only one who'd ever seen them, but that wouldn't make sense.

"Only if I shift forms, and that's not something I like doing around people." Seta's body sank lower into the water, finally covering her bare breasts I'd been doing my best to avoid staring at.

Unable to sit still, I scrubbed at my face. "Really? Most of the mermaids around campus seem to want to stay shifted as much as possible."

"Only because they are hoping to show off their bodies and catch your attention."

I barely heard her whispered words and barked a laugh. "That would be a shame."

Seta's scowl turned quizzical. "Why do you say that?"

Because there wasn't a single woman on earth as beautiful as the odd little mer in the water in front of me.

Because there was only one woman who'd ever captured my attention.

I didn't think this was the time for grand declarations, so I settled on, "Because they're wasting their time."

Standing, I adjusted myself as subtly as I could. The

floral perfume of Seta's desire still hung in the humid air, and as long as it was filling my lungs, I doubted my hard-on was going anywhere.

"Where's your stuff? Do you want me to put your clothes by the edge so you can change?"

"Um. Yeah?" Seta stammered.

When she bit her lip, I knew I needed to get away from her. I was teetering on the edge, fighting against the desire to explore her body with my mouth and find the source of her intoxicating nectar.

Grabbing her soaked clothing and the golden bangle I'd never seen her take off, I placed them on the pond's edge nearest her. "Here you go. They are a little wet. I'll go ahead and leave so you can have privacy."

My eyes drifted across her skin, and heat scorched through my body.

I had to go before I forgot my resolve to give her time before I confessed my growing feelings for her.

"Thank you, Deus. See you tomorrow?" Seta smiled up at me, causing thunder to pound in my ears and electricity to hum around me.

The storm inside me demanded release, and I couldn't do it here, not where I could hurt Seta.

Scratching at my tingling skin, I backed away. "Yeah. Tomorrow."

# CHAPTER 6
## SETA

The next two weeks were full of note-taking, paper-writing, pop quizzes, and lab experiments. It hadn't been too hard to memorize a dozen incantations, draw seven different diagrams for alchemical transformation, and write two practice papers for my academic writing class.

It had been harder to keep my eyes on my own books and ignore invitations to study groups and clubs. I was growing to like the staff and several of the other students. Which made it challenging to keep up the necessary, but almost rude, exterior I needed to deter people from trying to get closer to me.

Ayla finally gave up on inviting me along every time she left our room, but she was still determined to befriend me. She hadn't stopped giving me a full synopsis of her extracurricular activities whenever we returned to our room together, though.

The only time I was forced to be social was when working on the narwhal shifter project with Deus. Gorgeous, definitely off-limits Deus.

After the incident at the pond, it would've been easier if he'd let me handle the report alone. Then, I wouldn't be reminded of the way his touch had felt... both in my mind and in real life.

But he'd stubbornly ignored my request to let me do the project and had gamely looked through every bestiary volume in the library. He'd even color-coded his notes the same way I did mine.

When we presented our outline to Professor Mackenzie, his eyebrows raised so high they nearly merged with his hairline.

He'd looked from me to Deus and back again. "You've picked a heck of a first project. Have you two prepared a reading list?"

Deus handed his reading list over proudly, and I followed with mine. I had to hand it to Deus; he'd come prepared, and it made us both look good.

Professor Mackenzie looked through the lists, a small frown on his face. Looking up, he stared hard at Deus. "Tell me the difference between a narwhal shifter and a selkie."

"Uh, aside from the shape?" Deus grinned like it was a joke. "Selkies can remove their seal coats whenever they like. They don't become human by enchantment, and being human is part of their magical form. Narwhal shifters are shifters, which means they can take on a human form as part of the enchantment, but they're most comfortable as whales. And their horns do a lot of stuff, too."

"'A lot of stuff,'" Mackenzie echoed, shaking his head in bemusement before turning to me. "How much of that did you coach him to say?"

"Nothing," I replied honestly.

The professor's eyes narrowed, and his mouth thinned. He stared at me for a few seconds, but I refused to flinch. Finally, whatever test he was running on me, I evidently passed.

"I'm aware of your… special affinities for the sea, Seta." His tone made me wonder just *how* much he was aware of. "I never intended to go easy on you in this class. Doing a project like this will only make it harder for you to impress me."

"I can do it." I pushed my shoulders back and stood tall.

Mackenzie studied me for another moment before turning back to Deus. "And you? You'll share her grade, and I won't be merciful just because you're *not* a creature of the sea."

"I'm ready." Deus held out his fist for a bump. Mackenzie stared at it until Deus slowly lowered his hand.

Deus was adorable, but it took all my self-control to keep from face-palming.

"Fine. I'll put you down for narwhal shifters, but consider yourselves warned." Mackenzie shook his head at our foolishness and waved us away.

"Nice. Prof. Mackenzie thinks I'm an idiot, doesn't he?" Deus whispered as we left the classroom.

We had a study period now, making it the perfect time to crack open a book from our reading lists.

Sneaking a glance up at Deus's face, I caught the twitch of his lips.

Reluctantly, I pulled my eyes from his mouth and asked, "Why are you smiling?"

Technically, he always seemed to be smiling, but I wasn't sure why he was happy at the moment.

"I like proving people wrong about me." Deus smiled down at me. "Just like you. You think I want to spend all my time playing frisbee golf and tanning by the lake. Turns out I'm into narwhals, too. If I want to be."

"You *do* spend all your time on frisbee golf." I tried to distract myself from the mental image of a shirtless Deus lying on the grass by a sparkling lake.

"I do not." Deus bumped his shoulder playfully against mine.

He had no way of knowing that the simple touch had turned my insides to jelly or the way my skin begged for him to touch me again. What was wrong with me?

"Hey! Deus!" A gorgeous blonde waved from across the lawn, where she sat in a group of equally stunning females and circled by twice as many guys.

She flipped her bleach-blonde hair over her shoulder and smiled coyly. "Frisbee golf later?"

"Can't," Deus called back. Sticking his hands in his pockets, he grinned. "Anyway, frisbee golf is a great way to relax. If you spend all your time hunched over a desk, you'll get a backache."

He paused, thinking his own words over, then turned back toward the group. "How about four?"

"Deal." The girl turned back to her group, and a wave of giggles and high-fives broke out.

My stomach soured at the sound. *No nonsense*, I reminded myself. Deus could spend his time doing whatever he wanted with anyone he liked.

And honestly, anyone seemed to be *everyone*.

I'd never seen him alone with any of the female students, though. Which surprised me. We were all in our early twenties now, and I'd overheard enough bathroom and dining hall conversations to know many of the female students were here specifically to find a mate.

Shouldn't a hot catch like Deus have a girlfriend? Or maybe even a harem?

*Mine.*

I ignored the insistent inner voice that was growing possessive of Amadeus.

As we had settled into the semester and I started working on the narwhal shifter project with Deus in earnest, I'd seen just how many people liked to hang out with him. He was on a first-name basis with the whole academy. The student on the morning shift at the café gave him a latte on the house each morning, and Deus was on the automatic 'cool' list for every party, no matter how VIP.

Aside from the coffee—a landlocked thing I'd quickly come to love—the whole arrangement sounded horrific to me. I might long to be part of a small group of close friends, but the thought of everyone knowing my name was enough to make my tentacles curl.

Although, if the academy students ever realized what I truly was, I'd become as infamous as Deus was famous.

I had to admit, Deus took the attention with grace, and he gave as good as he got. When the coffee guy had flunked his Advanced Alchemy quiz, Deus had sat him down and listened patiently.

When his friend Ezric had been ghosted by the mermaid he'd been into, Deus had taken his phone and deleted her number. "You know it's for the best," he'd said gently and even gave Ezric a hug.

Deus was always inviting people to hang out with him. And honestly, it was exhausting. People stopped by every five minutes, whether we were in the dining hall, on the lawn, or in the library.

But I couldn't really blame them—Deus's aura was a cozy, glowing blanket, and the temptation to stop and snuggle was real.

Except I wasn't the snuggling type.

*Or at least I haven't been in the past…*

Eventually, I'd resorted to putting my headphones in whenever someone new popped by during our study sessions and drowned out their conversations.

Which is exactly what I'd been doing when Amadeus had plucked the headphones from my ears one day. We'd been seated in the library, and he'd just finished a lengthy chat with a girl who'd given him the tearful rundown of her grandmother's failing health.

I'd swiped out, trying to snag my headphones back, but Deus had dangled them out of my reach. "What are you always listening to, anyway?"

"Nothing." It had come out more defensive than I'd intended, so I'd added, "Ocean sounds."

"Really?" Deus had put the headphones on and listened for a few moments. He then popped one ear off. "It's really nice. Is it good for concentration?"

"It helps me relax." And reminded me of home and why I'd come all this way to do what I was doing. But I wasn't going to tell him all that.

"I get it." Deus had closed his eyes. "It has good movement. I bet it'd be good for… you know…" He'd opened an eye and gave me a sly look.

"What?" I'd asked, not catching his meaning.

Deus flashed me a tiny smile. I'd gotten to know him well enough by now to know that his small smiles were to hide his embarrassment. "You know. One-on-one time."

"This is one-on-one time. Or it would be if you stopped talking to every student on campus," I'd pointed out with a huff.

"Uh." He'd chuckled, two pink spots appearing on his cheeks.

I'd watched his face with fascination. I'd never seen him blush before.

"I mean a different sort of one-on-one time." That time, Deus hadn't met my eyes.

"Oh, sex." My matter-of-fact tone was loud enough that a group two tables away had looked over at us.

Deus had coughed and looked down at his book.

"I don't know if the rhythm would work, though—I mean, I don't have much experience with that."

"No? I'm surprised." Deus's eyebrows had risen.

"Why?" I'd asked, a little stung. Had he been sarcastic?

"Well, you're the most beautiful girl here, so I imagine you must've had no shortage of guys after you at home." He'd fiddled with the pages of *The Myth of the Unicorn*. There was a whole chapter in there on the difference between unicorn and narwhal horns.

"Oh my goddess," I'd muttered, feeling heat spread from my cheeks out to the tips of my ears. "Enough personal talk. We're going to study. Now."

Deus had smiled again, looking down at his book. That had been a smile with a closed mouth, one I'd learned to interpret as secretive.

I'd turned my attention to *Creatures of the North Atlantic*, but the words swam before my eyes and refused to make any sort of sense.

*He thinks I'm beautiful.*

He also seemed to think I'd had a lot of sexual experience.

Deus had leaned back. "Okay, I think I have something—"

"I'm not a sex addict!" I'd blurted.

He'd paused, his mouth open. "Uh, cool?"

My cheeks had flamed brighter than my hair. "I just wanted you to know."

He'd blinked several times before speaking. "So the narwhal's horn is better at detecting poison derived from a marine environment than a unicorn's horn, but a unicorn *shifter's* horn has no poison-detecting powers, and maybe that's a way to tell a narwhal shifter from a regular narwhal?"

Unfortunately, the floodgate had opened, and I was struggling to get it closed.

"It's just hard to get that kind of experience when the only guys my age are my cousins. I mean, how would you feel if the only people of... your kind... were related to you?"

Deus had paused again, looking lost for words for the first time since I'd met him.

He'd rubbed at his neck with one large hand and had shrugged those beautiful, broad shoulders. "Well, I have six brothers, and no one else in the world has our powers. So, I sort of get what you mean. Though there are a lot of mermaids and mermen around."

Right. I was a 'mermaid.'

"Not where I live," I'd tried to explain without revealing my secret. "And harpies are terrible kissers, and I don't want to know what else they're bad at, if you catch my wave."

"Coffee." Deus had stood, abruptly changing the subject. "Mocha. One for me and one for you."

"I don't need a mocha." It had been a lie, and we'd both known it. I loved mochas.

"Yes, you do. We both need coffee, and if we are going to get this report written, we probably need to forget this conversation."

He'd walked off, and I'd scrubbed my hands down my face. It had been frustrating giving into nonsense and equally frustrating that I hadn't been able to tell him everything.

If I didn't focus, there was no way I'd survive my Slaymore Academy experience.

WHEN DEUS RETURNED from getting our coffee, we dove straight back into our work, but I couldn't miss the way he kept fidgeting. His tongue darted out, sliding over his lips, and his ever-present smile kept shifting, like he didn't know what he wanted to say.

Finally, he took a deep breath. "Hey, Seta? I got you something."

He reached into his backpack and pulled out a gift bag. It was vibrant green and tied with gold ribbon.

Did other paranormals give each other presents for things like presentations? Was this a land-dweller tradition I wasn't aware of?

"I, uh… thanks?" I stammered, my brain telling my

heart that it wasn't personal. It didn't mean Deus felt anything for me.

Besides, I didn't want him to…

"Don't thank me 'til you've opened it," Deus joked.

I picked at the ribbon with shaking, uncooperative fingers. My belly twisted nervously. I'd never been given a gift from a guy. I was definitely in new territory here.

With a couple more tugs, the ribbon came free. I plucked out layers of white tissue paper until my hand closed around something smooth and hard. Pulling it free, I lifted it up to the light.

"*Epitonium scalare*," I gasped.

It was a pale pink shell, ribbed with white protrusions, its hollow body curling like a tower up to a point.

"Do you like it?" Deus's smile was anxious.

"I… You didn't kill some poor sea creature for this, did you?" I whispered.

"No!" He laughed. "Of course not. There's an antique shop here in town. I asked the owner what he had from the ocean. I figured, since mermaids like shells and coral, you might like this."

Deus looked so hopeful that it was all I could do not to laugh. I'd forgotten about that aspect of being a mermaid.

"I love it," I answered truthfully.

Mermaids liked pretty things, but Krakens took it to another level. We were the dragons of the sea, hoarding the treasures we collected.

It was beautiful and reminded me of the horns on the

narwhals we'd been studying. "Why... Why did you get it for me?"

One shoulder came up in a shrug, revealing a strip of bare collarbone beneath his shirt. His aura grew brighter, warmer.

"I wanted to impress you." His eyes dropped to the ground, not meeting mine.

The admission did weird things to my insides, and with my heart overruling logic, I threw my arms around his neck, toppling his chair. Deus caught me to his chest as he landed on his back.

"I guess you like it?" Deus's chest rumbled with laughter that vibrated through me.

I leaned forward. He smelled like sunlight. Sunlight and rain.

"Yes," I said.

Our mouths were inches apart, and up close, his eyes were as bottomless as the sea. Neither of us made a move to get up.

Memories of the night at the pond, his fingers tracing my imprints, my body still trembling from our imagined intimacy, filled me. I wanted more. I wanted it to be real.

Why couldn't I fall in love and still achieve my dreams? Why couldn't I have both? What I was feeling for Amadeus certainly didn't feel like nonsense. Maybe I'd been wrong to keep him at arm's length.

"What are you thinking?" Deus murmured, his warm breath ghosting across my lips.

"I'm smart. But at the same time, I'm not very smart," I admitted.

One hand came up to cup the back of my head. His thumb brushed over my lip. "Yeah?"

I read the invitation and the question in his single word.

"Yeah," I whispered.

Our mouths met.

This kiss was gentle, far softer than I'd expect from a guy who was made of lightning and storms. It was a heck of a lot softer than the savage kisses I'd experienced from the harpy boys.

Deus kept his hand at the back of my head, steadying me but letting me take the lead. I pressed in, letting our mouths meld together before brushing the tip of my tongue against his bottom lip.

As our tongues touched, a shock jolted down my spine.

I jerked back, breaking the kiss.

"Sorry." Deus's cheeks were red. "That's something I have to work on."

"Seems like something that practicing could help with," I teased before reality slammed into me like a freight train.

Every minute I was around him, the more my walls crumbled. Unless I wanted to fail my clan, I needed to clear my head and put distance between the gorgeous man beneath me and myself.

Scrambling off Deus's chest, I grabbed my backpack and his gift.

"See you tomorrow!" I called over my shoulder while rushing to the safety of my dorm.

# CHAPTER 7
## SETA

The next few days, I managed to keep my wits about me and not give in to the urges pushing me to throw myself at Deus. For his part, Deus was making it harder to resist falling for him just by being his sweet, thoughtful self.

Once he'd discovered how much I liked mochas, he brought one for each of us every time we met to work on our project. He claimed it helped with concentration, and maybe he was right since our slides were quickly filling with information.

I just hoped our project wasn't too basic for Professor Mackenzie.

Deus seemed just as invested as me and had reorganized every slide at least five times while also insisting I continue practicing my presentation skills.

"You can't just vomit out the words written on the slides. They have to flow. Just like when you speak. Think of it in ocean terms. Waves roll to shore, pull back, roll in a little further." Deus took a long swig from his water bottle.

I raised a brow. "Unless the tide's going out."

"It's not meant to be an exact metaphor." He gestured with a piece of sushi he'd snagged from the marine dining hall before meeting me on the lawn. "Come on. Presentations start tomorrow, and I want our slides to be perfect."

"They are perfect. Quit worrying." I picked at a blade of grass.

My skin was itching terribly. It had been five days since the last time I'd managed to sneak off to the pond for a swim. I felt grimy, and taking showers just wasn't enough.

With Deus wanting to pore over every detail of the project a million times, I was afraid he'd insist we meet again after dinner. I loved every minute I spent with him, but that would also mean I'd miss my chance for a swim tonight.

"They are not perfect until Professor Mackenzie says they are. Listen, I know you hate people, but you have to actually talk to them while you are presenting. You know that, right? We need to be ready." Deus's voice was gentle.

I swallowed back a groan of frustration. Deus had exceeded my expectations as a partner, but I couldn't wait until I obtained permission for independent study.

Not wanting to argue, I pasted a smile on my face and launched into the opening of the presentation. "We will be giving an overview of narwhal shifters, their habitats, feeding habits, and notable differences from both mundane narwhals and other paranormal marine life."

Deus nodded encouragingly, so I kept going, pushing my shoulders back and making sure I met his eyes—which wasn't easy.

The intensity of his piercing blue gaze felt like electricity crackling over my skin.

"Narwhals and narwhal shifters are native to the North Atlantic, with nomadic pods migrating between— Zeus on a stick, what *now*?"

Deus's attention had flicked away from me, and a grin split his face. That was the way he looked when someone was greeting him from afar.

*Great.* Another freaking interruption.

I turned to find Ezric standing in the shallows of the saltwater lake. He'd stripped to his shorts despite the cool, crisp fall day. The son-of-a-Kraken-hunter was the last person I wanted to see.

Ezric ran a hand through his hair, fluffing it into short, dark spikes. His eyes raked down my figure, and I got the absurd urge to fold my arms over my chest.

I glared at him instead, wishing I had my tentacles so I could flick him over backward without breaking a sweat.

"The water's refreshing. Come on in!" Ezric spread his arms invitingly.

"You know I don't do water." Deus laughed and focused his attention back in my direction. "Okay, what's next?"

"Bro." The grass rustled behind us as Ezric strode up. "Just to the knee. Isn't this part of your whole plan?

Besides, Alicia's in a strapless bikini. I promise you, it's worth getting wet for."

"Ugh," I muttered, flopping back onto the grass.

I hadn't meant for Ezric to hear, but he put a hand on his hip, just above his swimming trunks. "Need something, Red?"

*A break from you.* "We need to finish this presentation; thanks for asking," I growled.

"How's yours going, Ezric?" Deus asked, flashing me a small, grateful smile at the opportunity to change the subject.

Ezric lifted a shoulder. "Fine. My partner's in charge of the slides, and I'm in charge of the talking."

"I haven't seen you in class." I used my hand to block the sun from my eyes.

"That's because I have the afternoon periods," Ezric replied. "I have Advanced Combat in the morning block, and it couldn't be switched."

Advanced combat already? Only paranormals with particular gifts got to skip elementary combat classes. I filed the information away as potentially dangerous.

There was a loud splash from the direction of the lake. I sat up just as a girl—Alicia, presumably—did a perfect backflip out of the water.

Droplets spun from her body like sparkling diamonds. It was a stunning performance that only a marine paranormal could pull off.

Alicia resurfaced, water streaming down the strong

plane of her nose and her wide eyes brimming with mischief. "The water feels amazing today!"

I scratched my ribs. This was the worst kind of torture since I could practically taste the salt in the air. If I didn't get away from this lake in the next five minutes, I was going to go crazy.

"Take a break, man. You've done nothing but work on this project for the whole week," Ezric coaxed.

"Yeah, 'cause we're in bad shape," Deus said.

"We're in fine shape," I retorted, insulted at Deus's comment.

I'd done my fair share of the work and had double-checked all his information. I knew a good job when I saw one, and it rankled me that Deus doubted my abilities.

"See?" Ezric stretched, taking the opportunity to show off his pecs. "Even nerdy Ariel here says you're good to go. Come on, man. Face your fears! Isn't that what you wanted to do at Slaymore?"

Deus shifted. His eyes dropped to the ground, and his aura dimmed slightly.

I realized with a start that he was uncomfortable. How was that possible? Deus was never uncomfortable around people.

"In good time, man." Deus waved him away.

Ezric chuckled. "The lake's not getting any warmer."

"I'll take care of you, Deus." Alicia moved to the shallows and stood. She was a perfectly sculpted specimen of a woman. "You can swim out with me."

*MINE.*

"He said no thank you." My voice came out sharper than I'd intended, and Alicia's eyes narrowed as she truly looked at me for the first time.

"Did he, though?" Ezric put a finger on his sharp chin. "Did you say no, De?"

Deus's hand went to the back of his neck. "I mean, I could try."

Was that sweat beading on Deus's upper lip?

A cold breeze sent red and gold leaves chasing each other over the grass. I glanced up. Clouds were gathering where the sky had previously been blue.

"You obviously don't want to." I leaned toward Amadeus. "Just say no."

"He can't say no. Didn't he tell you? It's his weakness. And you might as well speak up. I'm a slayer." He tapped his ear. "Enhanced senses, all of them."

So that was Ezric's paranormal species. Cold flushed over my body. I'd already known his family hunted my kind, but I hadn't known what he was.

Many of my clan had lost their lives to slayers, making them the biggest risk to my species' long-term survival. Ezric was probably one of the students Headmistress Losia had warned me about.

He smiled at Deus, and maybe it was because I was starting to think of him as a world-class dick, but the smile seemed cold and cruel.

"We need to finish this presentation, Deus. Come on." I stood up, closing my laptop.

The library was probably full of people at that hour, but

maybe I could convince Ayla to let us hang out in the dorm room.

At least I knew that she, the self-proclaimed sexless succubus, wouldn't be throwing herself at Deus in a strapless bikini.

Deus seemed only too happy to scramble to his feet. "Uh, yeah. I mean, sure. If you feel you need to practice more."

I rolled my eyes. I was saving his adorable arse, yet he thought he could pretend he was some kind of helping hero?

Ezric's smile flattened. He watched Deus pick up his books, stacking them neatly. As Deus got to his feet and slung his backpack over his shoulder, Ezric plucked a book from the top of the pile.

"*Shifters of the Arctic*," Ezric read aloud. "Any good?"

"It's kinda dry, actually. But it had some— *Hey!*"

Ezric drew back his arm and hurled the book. Deus's books tumbled from his arms as he leaped after it. But his effort was futile. The book spun through the air, skipped twice over the surface of the lake, and sank.

Deus turned to Ezric, his mouth agape. For the first time, there was no hint of easy-going geniality on his face. "What the heck, man? That's a library book."

Sharp, gold light seemed to radiate from his skin. It was so bright and prickling that I found myself looking away from Deus.

"So go get it, Golden Boy. It'll dry off." Ezric smirked.

Deus looked to the lake, then back at Ezric.

This was why I didn't do friends. They were a serious pain in the tush. Shoving past Ezric, I stomped over to the lake.

I kicked off my sneakers and rolled up my sleeves. My skin tingled, warning me that this was a spectacularly bad idea. I wanted to release my true form too much.

But I was finished watching Deus get bullied by his so-called friend and finished wasting my time as other people tried to flirt with my partner—my project partner.

Yeah, that was it. I was annoyed that they kept distracting us from our work… it had nothing to do with the weird feelings Amadeus seemed to stir inside me.

"I can get it." Alicia stood in the shallows, her face stricken as she looked toward the two guys having an alpha showdown.

"Oh, now you want to help?" I snapped.

Her eyes cut to me, and her lip curled in disgust.

I didn't care because I was finished with her, too.

She should've accepted Deus's first *no*, but his comfort was apparently less important than her desire to have an opportunity to feel him up.

The water hit my toes, and I gasped.

I stopped in the shallows, fighting the overwhelming desire to release my tentacles and bask in the glorious saltwater.

The water washed coolly over my toes. Even with just my feet submerged, I could feel everything—the fish, a handful of crabs, and the single squid shifter that had taken refuge at the lake's deepest point. A sleek barracuda and a juvenile sea serpent played among strands of seagrass on the lake's far side.

I touched my cuff, reassuring myself it was still there.

With it on my wrist, I'd only reveal myself if I wanted to. And I didn't want to, right?

*Right.*

That would be really stupid with Ezric, the slayer, watching me from the lake's edge.

# CHAPTER 8
## SETA

I waded into the cool water, heedless of my jeans or my black button-up shirt. Every step into the salty liquid was a blissful type of torture.

My shifter side begged for me to release us so we could dive to the bottom and stay there until presentation time tomorrow. Actually, forget the presentation—I wanted to stay there forever.

*Nonsense.* What was I thinking? I'd already let myself become distracted by my body's reactions to Amadeus. Now, I was letting my need for water distract me from my assignment.

That presentation was my whole reason for being on land… at least until my next project. This was my ticket to impressing Professor Mackenzie, which would hopefully get me straight into the advanced marine classes next semester.

Heck, this presentation might even give me a leg up on my crusade to be allowed to study independently.

Ducking under the water, I repeated my plan.

Get the book.

Get an A tomorrow.

Go to Headmistress Losia's pond and marinate for the rest of the weekend.

Thankfully, the book was an easy find, having become stuck in the silt about eight feet down. Basic enchantments protected it from accidents like coffee spills, so it was less waterlogged than a normal book would be.

Still, Deus and I would be practicing incantations tonight to clean it up if he didn't want to face a hefty library fine later. I grabbed the book, took one last regretful look at the bottom of the lake, and kicked up toward the surface.

I swam in easy strokes back to the edge of the lake. As I emerged from the lake, the cold air whipped at my wet shirt, and the sting of it was almost enough to drive me back beneath the water.

But I wasn't sure I'd be able to contain my tentacles if I took a second swim. Plus, I needed to run back to my dorm room and change.

"Sorry," Alicia said softly as I walked past her.

I appreciated the apology, but I was still too annoyed at how they'd pushed against Deus's boundaries to reply.

My jeans dragged on my hips, forcing me to haul them up with one hand while clutching the book in my other.

Shoving my wet feet back into my shoes, I stalked over to Deus.

His aura softened as I approached, and the warmth that surrounded him momentarily banished the brisk fall air. "Let me get your bag."

Ezric's eyes were going over my figure again. This time, though, he wasn't leering or appraising. He was watching me like a hunter assessing a threat.

"What's that?" He pointed at my wrist.

My cuff was glowing a pale blue, probably with the effort of keeping my true form subdued.

"None of your business," I snarled as we went by him.

"Hey, I'm just asking. No need to be a brat," he called at my back.

Just asking, my arse. "If you want me to be nice, you could start by not throwing our project resources into a lake."

"Seta, hang on." Deus panted, trotting after me. "Seta, slow down. I've got two bags here and a ton of books—"

"I'll slow down when I'm dry," I replied in a tone so final that Deus stopped talking and followed me inside.

Ayla was out, *thank Poseidon*.

I wasn't in the mood for half a dozen questions and a long conversation between the two chattiest people I knew.

"Make yourself comfortable. I'm going to change." Grabbing my pajamas, I went into the bathroom.

I slung my wet clothes over the shower rail and wrapped my hair in a towel. Heading back into the bedroom, I found Deus sitting on my bed.

He was looking at Ayla's half of the room with interest. The ever-present smile was back. Deus had put my bag down next to my desk, and the soggy library book rested on top of it.

"Is your roommate an artist?" He pointed to the sketches Ayla had pinned to her side of the wall.

"Yes, she's very talented."

We remained quiet for several minutes. My mind kept replaying the scene at the lake with Ezric, and my annoyance began to grow.

"You are the nicest person I've ever met, Deus. But how is it you know every word in the English language except for no?"

His smile and aura dimmed. "I like helping people out. Trying to see things from their point of view, et cetera."

"That doesn't mean you have no boundaries. Come on, Deus. You're terrified of the water, but you were going to let your dick friend push you into getting in? Knowing you could electrocute everything?" If I were in my true form, my irritation would be creating whirlpools.

"Come on. Ezric's an okay guy." Deus ruffled his curly mane.

"You're changing the subject. And no, he's not," I replied firmly. "Ezric knows you don't like the water."

I held my tongue to keep from adding that Ezric was also delighted with the slaughter of another species, so how okay could he be?

"Maybe he was just trying to help me better myself?"

Deus put his palms out, still trying to find the good in people.

"I can't believe you made it twenty years without learning to say no." With a huff, I flopped down on the edge of the bed beside Deus.

Lifting the cover of *Shifters of the Arctic*, I inspected the water damage. We'd covered paranormal-specific spells in Basic Incantations, so I'd already researched how to dry something I might have left in my pocket by accident.

Unfortunately, I'd never tried the incantation on anything bigger than a pen, and that hadn't gone exactly to plan; I'd dried out the ink and ruined the pen.

"I'm a people pleaser. I know it's a problem. I just..." He sighed.

Deus leaned back against the wall, and I watched slack-jawed as the golden light around him mellowed, and an invisible cloak seemed to fall away from him. It was as though Deus was dropping an act—the act of being happy for everyone all the time.

"You've seen my power." He held up one hand, and white light flashed between his fingers. "We've gone over how dangerous it is. Well, my brothers were always competitive. They wanted to see who could make the biggest thunderclap or the most strikes in a minute."

Deus closed his eyes. "There were so many times when they thought it was funny to scare people with our abilities. It didn't bother my brothers, but it bothered me. I never wanted people to be afraid of me. So I'd go out of my way to help them instead, so they always knew they could count on me. My brothers loved being the storm, but I'd rather be the shelter."

My heart ached at his words because I didn't want to be feared, either. How far would I go to ensure Krakens were understood as the complicated, gentle creatures we were? Rather than the fearsome, mindless monsters bent on destroying lives?

"Deus, you can't put your own needs last." I kept my voice gentle, not wanting to seem harsh.

When he didn't respond, I shifted onto my knees and scooted against his side. "You almost hurt yourself, and for what? So you could flirt a bit with a girl and keep your friend happy?"

Deus opened one cerulean blue eye and looked at me. "Who do you think I was flirting with?"

"The mermaid. Er, I mean, the *other* mermaid," I hastily amended.

"Ha." His laugh was dry, and he closed his eyelid again. "No, I wasn't."

"Well, she was flirting with you. And you were acting like you wanted to impress her." I tried to keep an accusing tone from my voice.

Deus snorted. "Why would I want to impress her?"

Because she has perfect skin, and perfect thighs, and a perfect belly. Did he want me to spell it out? Why wouldn't a guy want to impress her?

Secretly, I was finding his lack of interest, well… nice.

"Maybe because she is the most eligible girl on the

campus, from what Ayla has told me?" The words were bitter on my tongue.

I told myself it was simply because I could barely handle Deus being Slaymore's most popular single guy and that it had nothing to do with the fact I secretly wanted him to be *my* guy.

Besides, it would be horrible to work on joint projects if he had a girlfriend attached to his hip. Especially if we had to stop working on them to kiss every five minutes…

Warm hands circled my waist, lifting me from the bed and settling me astride his hips.

"Seta, you are the most stubborn woman I've ever had the pleasure of meeting." My shirt had ridden up, and Deus's thumbs brushed my bare skin. "Let me spell this out for you. I can't see any of the other girls at Slaymore because I can't pull my eyes away from you."

"Deus…" Tears burned the back of my eyes.

I knew I should stop this before it went too far. No attachments was what I claimed to want, but that lie was beginning to crumble. Remaining still, I drank in his words and touch.

"I'm drawn to you in a way I didn't think I'd ever experience. And at the risk of you thinking I'm crude"—Deus held my hips as he ground his hips against me, allowing me to feel his stiff erection—"I want you."

Amadeus wanted me. My breath was coming in shallow pants.

Unable to resist, I slid my arms around his neck and rocked against him, causing us to gasp in unison.

"Seta," Deus groaned, and his hands slid beneath my shirt, brushing my ribcage.

I should move away.

*Mine.*

Shifting my hips on his lap, I moaned at the tiny ripple of pleasure the motion created.

"You're so unbelievably beautiful. I want to touch you." Deus's blue eyes flashed.

Now was the time to stop this nonsense and focus on the important things, but I wasn't going to stop.

"Then touch me." Leaning forward, I placed a featherlight kiss on Deus's mouth.

That was all it took for his hands to continue their exploration while our hips moved in a perfect rhythm. We were college students who were humping like horny high school kids, but it felt too incredible for me to care how ridiculous the situation might be.

When Deus's fingers brushed the underside of my breast, I whimpered, arching into his touch. My body sent a wave of slick need between my thighs, and my stomach clenched with building need.

Deus caught my mouth in a searing kiss, his hands moving to cup my breasts. From there, things turned into a frenzy of groping hands, grinding hips, and dancing tongues.

My insides were twisting tighter and tighter as my hunger for release grew stronger. Amadeus's radiant glow was back and brighter than ever. It enveloped me in its warmth, even as static crackled across our skin.

"Deus?" I panted.

"Yes?" he murmured between kisses on my neck.

"If we don't stop now, I'm going to..." My cheeks burned. "I'm going to climax."

"Come for me." Deus's teeth nipped the skin of my collarbone. "Use me."

Wrapping my arms tighter around his neck, our movements became harder and faster.

*Mine.*

At least for this brief moment, he was mine. Breathing in his smoky scent, I tried to commit every sensation to memory.

When his fingers teased my nipples, I fell apart, clinging to him as orgasmic pleasure shredded every fiber of my being. I'd thought imaginary sex with Deus had been amazing, but although we were both still clothed, this was far better.

I was also even more sure that I'd never survive actual sex with this man.

Deus held me while tremors shook my body, his hips thrusting against me several more times before he stiffened.

"Seta," Deus hissed between clenched teeth, his arms clamping around me and pinning me to his chest.

Through my thin pajama shorts, I could feel the scorching heat of Deus's cock jerking with his release. Intense pride swelled in my chest. He wanted me just as much as I craved him.

*Mine.*

I lay against his chest, listening to his heartbeat and

finding it almost as relaxing as the soundtrack of the sea I played on repeat.

"I can't believe that just happened." Deus gave a tense laugh. "I swear I'm not a hormonal teen who comes apart at a single touch. You affect me in ways I don't understand."

Sitting up, I gave him a soft kiss on the cheek. "It was perfect. Every bit of it."

Not ready to discuss what had happened between us and not wanting Ayla to find me straddling Deus, I adjusted my clothing and slid from his lap.

"I hate to ruin the moment, but we should probably see if we can fix this before tomorrow." I picked up the damaged book and gave him a cheeky grin. "You can go clean up in the bathroom, and I'll get started."

# CHAPTER 9
## SETA

Mackenzie called us up to present first the following afternoon. We'd practiced our presentation twice more the night before, and I'd even added a few follow-up questions from the perspective of the audience. Mackenzie had said he wouldn't go easy on us, and we weren't taking any chances.

Deus shot me a nervous glance as we headed to the front of the class, and I returned it with what I hoped was a professional-looking and encouraging smile. Other than a little stumble on Deus's part in the first portion of the introduction, things went fairly smoothly.

I tried to remember all the things Deus had coached me on—eye contact with the class, no fiddling, and trying to look friendly instead of looking like I had a stick up my arse.

We finished and received the lackluster applause that was typical of every group project presentation.

"Does anyone have questions for Amadeus and Seta?" Professor Mackenzie asked.

Silence.

"No questions? Fine, I've got one." The professor leaned back against his desk. "What makes you assume that narwhal shifters' horns have no special powers?"

I was ready to answer, but glanced at Deus since it had been his slide.

"We, uh…" Deus cleared his throat, lifting his hand to scratch the back of his neck. "We didn't assume that, sir. We think it's possible that narwhal horns don't have the same properties as a narwhal shifter's horn. It makes more sense, given that unicorn horns and unicorn shifter horns are also different. But there's a lack of evidence either way."

Mackenzie's eyes sparkled in what I hoped was approval. "Thank you. Come see me after class for your grade. Next up, Tricia and Waden."

The rest of the hour dragged by as we sat through several presentations. Deus tapped a rhythm on the desk, his fingers crackling with so much energy he left the occasional star-shaped scorch mark on the wood.

"It will be fine. Stop stressing," I whispered, grabbing his wrist to stop his anxious fidgeting.

Deus twisted his arm around, intertwining his fingers through mine. He gave a gentle squeeze, and my heart jolted.

I looked down at my own desk, focused on my notes, and tried not to think about how good his fingers felt sliding against mine. It was comfortable, but at the same time, his touch made me hyper-aware of every inch of space that separated us.

I'd gone from trying to maintain an ice-queen persona to fighting against the urge to cling to Deus. There was no denying I was losing the battle. I was going to need to figure out if there was a way I could accomplish my goals and have Deus.

When the bell rang at last, we stayed behind and watched Mackenzie dole out grades to the other groups. I didn't want to let go of Deus's hand just yet, but when everyone else had filed out, we shuffled to the front.

"Seta and Amadeus." Mackenzie folded his arms and smiled. "Ninety-eight. Very good."

"Yes!" Deus hissed.

I chewed on my lip. "What happened to the other 2 percent?"

Deus's eyes widened. "Seta!"

"I took off the points because you looked a tad uncomfortable up there. Relax, be confident in yourselves. Then you'll earn your full marks." Mackenzie looked between us. "I have to admit, I'm impressed. You picked a difficult topic that isn't well published in the academic world, and you were able to do quite a lot with it. It was clear you both worked hard. Seta, even with your natural advantages, you went above and beyond. The two of you work well together, and I look forward to seeing what you bring me next."

The professor's words took root inside of me, growing until I thought I'd burst with pride at his praise. I didn't even try to stifle my smile as we thanked him and set off to enjoy the rest of our day.

"You know he's going to want us to top that with the next project, right?" Deus stuck his hands in his pockets, his shoulders relaxing for the first time that morning.

I already had another project in mind, but it was one I wanted to present for independent study.

"Well done, partner," I said, turning toward the dormitory. "It was a pleasure."

Deus laughed. "Where are you going?"

My mood dimmed slightly, and I grumbled, "Alchemy homework." It was my least favorite course.

"We don't have alchemy 'til Monday. Come on." He reached down and grabbed my hand, acting as though it were natural and something we did all the time. "We're celebrating!"

"I'm tired of socializing." I dug in my heels.

"You'll enjoy this. I promise." The gentle glow of Deus's skin, the mischievous glint in his blue eyes, the sexy smile on his lips—all worked to unravel my resolve, and it whipped away on the wind as though it were nothing more than sea foam.

I let him lead me down the gravel path toward the back of Slaymore's Victorian layer-cake-style administrative building. But instead of going inside, he took me around the side, through a grouping of birch trees that bent over the path, creating a tunnel.

Wind whipped through the branches, and I held my sweater closed. "Where are we going?"

"When was the last time you went off campus?" he asked.

Off campus? I didn't realize Slaymore students were allowed to visit places off campus.

"Stop frowning." Deus chuckled. "You're really going to like this!"

We emerged from the birch onto a narrow cobblestone road that was lined on either side by a brick wall. A tall gate shimmered with magic at the end of the path, and beyond it, I spotted a long row of quaint shops.

Amadeus placed a hand on the gate and pushed. "It only opens if there aren't any mundanes around to see it," he explained. "And once we're out here, no form shifting."

"Obviously." I rolled my eyes but surreptitiously checked that my cuff was in place, and we stepped out.

When I'd passed Slaymore village on my way to the academy, I hadn't given it much thought. Every place on land seemed mundane compared to the wonders of the sea, so I'd never considered it might have shops that appealed to me. But after spending more time on land, I had to admit the half-timber houses were cute.

They were painted in chipper yellow and blue hues, and each house was bursting with fall flowers in gardens and window boxes. Most of them appeared to have shops on the bottom floor and living areas on top.

We walked past a plant nursery, a jeweler, and a baker before Deus stopped in front of a leaning, three-story house. *Books and Brews*, the swinging metal sign shaped like a book declared.

"Coffee and books." Deus's fingers tightened on mine. "Tell me this isn't better than alchemy homework."

I couldn't hide my grin as I pushed open the front door and was greeted by the smell of paper and roasting coffee. The front room held a long bar with a pastry case and an espresso machine.

Two tiny circular tables were squeezed into the space, and a window well had been padded with cushions to make a cozy reading nook. Potted plants hung from the ceiling and decorated the bookcases to either side of the bar.

"Amadeus!" the rosy-cheeked woman at the bar greeted with a beaming smile.

I rolled my eyes. Of course she knew him.

She had a riot of black curls she kept out of her face with a headband, a proud nose, and kind, violet eyes that matched her wrap dress.

"And I haven't met you before." The woman worked as she talked, rinsing out milk pitchers and wiping up coffee grounds.

She gave off such a no-nonsense air that I couldn't help but like her. "Here's the deal. You tell me what you like to read and what you want to drink. I'll make your coffee and bring you a book."

"Cool, right?" Deus whispered. "And Marita's a witch, so everything she brews is pretty much magical."

My surprise must have shown on my face, because Marita burst into laughter.

"It's a mundane town, but us paranormals have to live somewhere. I teach the advanced witchery classes at Slaymore, but I don't guess you're a witch since I haven't met you," she said shrewdly.

"Mermaid." Repeating the lie was getting easier, but I still didn't like it.

I gave her my coffee order and asked for a fantasy novel. With a nod, she ground the beans, steamed the milk, and swirled it three times before pouring it counterclockwise into my glass. We all watched closely as the milk speckled the espresso.

"Got it. Take a seat, and I'll be right back with your book." She bustled off, leaving us to take the window seat.

For once, I was happy to let the sun warm my face as I leaned back against the aging wallpaper. "I can't believe there's no one else in here."

"You'll have to catch it on the off days if you want the place to yourself," Deus said. "Personally, I like coming in to see the people."

"Of course you do." I took a sip of white chocolate mocha.

Marita reappeared, handing me a leather-covered novel. "Anything for you, Deus? Otherwise, I have some restocking to do upstairs."

Deus's eyes cut to me, and that full mouth twisted. "I'll be right back."

My fingers drummed on the cover of my book as I watched him head to the bar. Getting a boyfriend hadn't been part of my plan.

In fact, my mother's insistence on me being mated as quickly as possible had driven out any desire to pursue a relationship. But I couldn't deny I was dying to feel his lips against mine again… and possibly more.

*Stop it, Seta.*

What proof did I have that Deus wanted anything more than a casual fling? And in all honesty, what was wrong with having one?

We studied well together, and it seemed like we might do other things well, too. As long as I kept up my grades, there was no reason I shouldn't enjoy my time on land. And right now, I wanted to enjoy my book, my coffee, and my guy.

Smiling into my mug, I had to admit my first semester at Slaymore was going swimmingly well.

I WAS eager to start the next marine mythology project right away but was forced to acknowledge the existence of my other classes at Slaymore. Writing academic papers was something I could do in my sleep, and I knew I'd be getting an A in all my courses at the end of the semester.

There was only one class that made me work harder.

Alchemy.

"I bet you could turn these into an art project." Ayla held up a pebble I'd been trying to transform into a sapphire.

"*You* turn them into an art project," I muttered, rubbing my temples and squinting at my notes.

I'd been at this stupid assignment for three hours, and I still couldn't figure out where I'd gone wrong. My notes were starting to blur together.

"May I? I'm trying to cheer up a friend. You remember Helena, who I told you about?" She launched into a soliloquy about the trials of her friend Helena.

I zoned out as I stared dully at my latest pebble, a simple piece of granite I'd snagged on a trip to *Books and Brews*. If I could just manage to turn it to quartz...

Ayla's voice cut into my thoughts. "—Ezric, so now half the academy knows."

"Ezric?" My head snapped up. "Ezric the slayer?"

Ayla rolled her eyes. "I prefer using his other name—Tall, Dark and Douchy. The dude really has a hard time taking no for an answer."

"I know another guy with the same issue," I said absently, rolling the pebble between my fingers.

"Are you talking about Amadeus Koidos?" She jolted up, staring at me under the fringe of bangs she'd cut in front of our bathroom mirror the night before. "I know you were paired with him for a project, but are you hanging out with him?"

More like on top of him, pressing against him as though we were trying to meld our skins together.

My cheeks burned. "Uh, yeah."

"Oh my goddess, you have a *crush* on him," Ayla gasped.

I let my hair fall in front of my face, trying to hide my telltale blush.

"Seta, he's like your exact opposite!" She clapped her hands together. "He is so *perfect* for you. Have you told him how you feel?"

"I plead the fifth." I set my books on the floor and scooted under my covers. If she wasn't going to let me study my alchemy, I might as well get some sleep.

"Seta, you can *not* leave me hanging like that!"

"Yes, I can." I playfully stuck out my tongue and reached for my headphones.

Ayla was used to my introverted ways by now and had grown good at ignoring my boundaries and protests.

She fluttered her eyelashes. "Have you two kissed yet?"

Ignoring the question, I lay down and stretched out. It had taken long enough, but I was getting used to human beds, though studying until I was exhausted helped, too.

"Fine, be a meanie."

I cracked open an eyelid and caught Ayla's exaggerated pout and twinkling eyes. "So, do you want help doing your hair tomorrow? I can help you with a dress, or paint your nails, or—"

"I'll think about it." I smiled and let her voice fade away as the sounds of the ocean filled my ears.

"Come study with me," Amadeus offered when I confided my alchemy frustrations to him. "I've got a whole group that studies together. We do alchemy, academic writing, philosophy of combat—"

"I study best on my own."

We were stretched out in the window seat at *Books and Brews*, which meant I had to sit and talk like a self-respecting adult instead of doing what I really longed to do —cling to him like an octopus... or more accurately, like a Kraken.

The man was wearing a tight-fitting navy tee, and his glow was giving him the 'magical tan' that made his perfect teeth seem even whiter.

"I know." He gave me an indulgent smile over the top of his latte macchiato. "But someone might have a method that speaks to you. Rock transformations will be part of the midterm exam, for sure."

"I know." Groaning, I let my head thump back against the wall. "I can recite the principles back to front, but my practical abilities suck."

"Knowing the principles will get you a C, at least," Deus pointed out. "Professor Farrious said you could pass the class without being able to do even a bit of practical alchemy."

My lips thinned. "I don't get C's."

I scowled at him as I took a bite of the croissant he'd insisted on buying for us to share.

"Right." Deus laughed. "How could I forget you're hardcore?"

"If I recall correctly, you were quite willing to do the extra work to get an A in the marine mythology project," I teased, bumping our knees together.

Deus's leg slid along mine, sending tingles up my whole body. "Sure, I like getting good grades. But if I did my best and got a C, I'd be fine with that."

I tossed back the last of my coffee. "Let's take a walk."

With Deus so close, I couldn't stop my mind from running wild. I imagined pinning him down with my tentacles. Would it be possible to take his shirt off with my teeth? I wasn't sure, but I was dying to try.

Hopefully, the fresh air would get my mind back on alchemy, and even if it didn't, it would definitely help get some of this pent-up energy out.

We made our way back to Slaymore grounds. As soon as we went through the gate, he sighed and held out his hand. A small bolt of lightning shot from his palm to the ground, leaving a scorched path of grass beside the path.

"I always need to let out some of this erratic electricity

when I come back from the mundane world," he explained, intertwining his fingers back through mine.

I wished I could slip my bracelet off and dive into the lake to ease the discomfort of maintaining this form around the clock. Every few days, I managed to sneak away to the freshwater pond, but within hours, I was once again hungry for the feel of water on my skin.

Deus must have read the wistfulness on my face. "Do you want to go to the lake? I can watch while you swim."

"No, thanks." I pulled him through the arching birch trees. "It's full of mermaids."

Leaves rustled as we kicked our way through them, and Deus laughed. "Isn't that sort of the point? You've got to be the least sociable mermaid I've ever met. I thought you guys were communal creatures?"

"My clan is... different." As in, so different we weren't even mermaids. "We prefer solitude."

"Well, I'm glad you came out of your self-imposed solitude to hang out with me," he teased.

"Me too," I said, tilting my head up to the gray sky. "A distraction is just what I need to de-stress."

"A distraction?" Deus sounded surprised.

I hesitated, trying to pick my words carefully. What if I admitted it was more than a distraction to me, but he didn't feel the same? "That's what this is, isn't it?"

"Well, we've never talked about it..." His voice was carefully neutral, not giving me a hint as to what he was thinking.

I stopped, forcing him to turn toward me or let go of my hand. He turned.

Deus wasn't smiling anymore, but he wasn't frowning, either.

"You know my academic learning is important to me." I swallowed hard. "I can't lose focus on my reasons for coming here."

"I'd never ask that of you." Deus tucked a stray bit of hair behind my ear.

"I like… this," I admitted, gesturing between us. "I was determined I wouldn't get distracted by romance, but I'd like to see where this goes."

One side of Deus's mouth turned up in a half-smile, and my face blazed with heat.

"But I also want it casual. Poseidon knows my mother has tried to brainwash me into mating instead of chasing my dreams, and I refuse to give up on my goals. We can hang out, we can read, we can…" I wasn't good at talking dirty or coming up with sly euphemisms. And when Deus stepped closer, I found I wasn't really all that great at making sentences at all.

"We can study?" he suggested, his hand finding my waist.

He stepped forward again, this time guiding me backward off the path and between the trees.

"That's not what I was going to say," I admitted, my blood growing warmer with each step.

My back hit a birch trunk.

"But I like studying with you." Deus caught both my hands in one of his and lifted my arms above my head.

Up close, I could see the stubble that had grown on Deus's jaw since he'd shaved this morning, and it was silly how sexy I was finding it.

"I like studying you." Deus nuzzled my neck. "For example, did you know you have a freckle right *here*?" He moved to place a sensuous kiss right under my ear, sending a wave of desire rolling through me.

*Mine.*

I let my eyes flutter closed as Deus began kissing his way down my neck, his tongue flicking at my skin.

"Wait," I gasped, and he froze. As much as I wanted this to be something more, I just couldn't allow myself to go down that road. "Deus, are you sure you're okay with the whole 'casual' thing?"

He was motionless, and my stomach quivered.

Finally, Deus spoke. "If that is what you want, then yes, I can do casual."

If his voice seemed a little off its usual happy lilt, I didn't have time to analyze it before his mouth began to move.

Deus released my hands, and I brought my arms around his shoulders. My shirt rode up, and he quickly took advantage of it. His hands slipped beneath my top, moving up my stomach and toward my breasts.

I tangled my fingers in his hair, my lips kissing whatever I could reach—his jaw, his neck, his ear.

Deus's breathing grew rough, and I took that as encouragement. I wrapped one leg around his waist, then the other. One of his hands moved to cup my butt while the other brushed across the bottom of my breast.

"Is this all right?" he breathed.

"No." I squirmed against him. "You're teasing me."

When his eyes met mine, they were feverish, and his smile was wild. "I don't mind that."

Then, our mouths clashed together. I clung to him, my tongue dancing with his. Deus groaned, and I could feel his hardness pressing against me. I loved knowing *I* had done that... I'd stirred desire and lust in him.

My thong was growing wet, and an ache was growing between my thighs. I squeezed my legs tighter around him.

"You've one heck of a grip," Deus whispered against my mouth.

"Sorry." I loosened my hold.

From the corner of my eye, I caught the blue glow of my cuff. The magic was working overtime to keep me from shifting, and I hadn't even been aware of wanting to release my tentacles. It must have been a side effect of my arousal.

"Don't be sorry. I'm into it." He shifted me against the tree.

And then he was kissing me again, and I forgot to worry about anything. About my alchemy grade, about my tentacles, about what we were or why I thought he was mine, and about what we were doing.

Nothing mattered except living in this moment with Amadeus.

When Deus's thumb brushed my nipple, I gasped, my body automatically arching into him—

Sound exploded above us, the scent of hot sap and smoke filling my nose. A jolt of adrenaline shot through my body, and I screamed in surprise.

A second later, it began to rain.

I looked up through the tree canopy above us. The sky had gone from gray to black over our heads, and the downpour seemed focused on us. It soaked my hair, clothes and the birch tree behind us, but I could see dry ground just ten feet away.

Twisting my neck, I studied the birch's bark above us. It was black and smoldering. My mouth fell open, and I turned to ask Deus what was going on, only to find he was smoldering, too.

Literally.

Steam rose from his skin, and his body had grown unbelievably hot.

Deus ran a shaking hand through his hair. "I'm sorry—I'm so sorry, Seta. I have *got* to work on controlling that."

I knew I should have been more freaked out by the fact the guy I'd just been kissing had blown up the tree we were standing beneath and, had the lightning hit a few feet lower, I'd be BBQ'd Kraken. Strangely enough, I hadn't felt this safe since I'd arrived on land. It made no sense, but I knew in my tentacles that he'd never hurt me.

*Because he's mine, and I'm his.* I wanted to facepalm.

*Way to keep things casual, Seta.*

"A bit of water has never bothered me." I grinned,

hoping to lighten the mood, and arched a brow. "Maybe I'm too much to handle?"

"It's hard to control my electricity when I have Slaymore's most beautiful girl wrapped around my body like a tight-fitting glove." Deus adjusted his jeans. "You're already soaked. I'll take you home so you can dry off."

I was soaked in more ways than one, and the last thing I wanted was to go back to my room. But Deus seemed shaken, so I nodded and let him lead me through the woods to the dorm.

# CHAPTER 10
## SETA

"You *sneak!*" Ayla squealed gleefully and tossed a pillow at me as I walked through the door. "You've been kissing Amadeus Koidos, and I had to find out through Alicia Moss?"

Ayla wore a silver metallic mini dress and lipstick a hue of purple so deep it was nearly black. She was clearly on her way to a party.

I winced, motioning for her to be quiet. "Keep it down, Deus is still in the hall!"

"Girl, you are so devious. And here I was trying to give you tips on how to nab him! Now we have to talk about how you keep him."

"What makes you think I want to do that?" I shucked my clothes and reached for my pajamas.

"Um, the fact that he's Amadeus?" Ayla said it as though I were crazy. "Half of Slaymore is in love with him."

"So? Half the school's in love with you too," I pointed out, unzipping my bag and beginning to remove my notebooks.

The Deus-induced storm had been brief and, thankfully, nothing was wet.

Ayla wagged a finger. "Half the school wants to sleep with me, but that's only because I'm a magical sex machine. It's not the same thing."

"Maybe Amadeus is a magical sex machine. Ever think of that?"

"You know that's not the same— Wait." Ayla's jaw dropped, revealing perfect white teeth. "Did you just make a *joke*? Seta sa Bering, are we becoming friends?"

"No," I said, struggling to keep from smiling.

Ayla was across the room and squeezing me in a bear hug before I dodge her. "Yes, we are! I knew you couldn't resist my awesomeness forever!"

"Yeah, fine. Whatever." I gently disentangled myself from Ayla's grasp. "But don't go telling everyone. I prefer being left alone… in case you hadn't noticed."

Ayla and Deus had made it past my barriers, and I was secretly pleased to have them in my life. But it was time to get back to focusing on my assignments, and figuring out how to pass alchemy with a perfect score.

"We will be talking about this later." Ayla winked and waltzed across the room to grab her tiny clutch. "And we will definitely be going over date ideas. I know succubi are mainly known for our sexcapades, but we are insanely talented when it comes to romance, too."

Ayla pointed two fingers at her eyes and then at me. "Tomorrow morning, brunch, you and me."

Tomorrow was Saturday, which meant the library would be empty and I could sit anywhere I wanted. The perfect study time. "No. I can't—"

She opened the door and blew me a kiss over her shoulder. "Trust me."

I grumbled under my breath as I settled at my desk and started drawing a new transformation chart for my pebbles. Deus had given me a few suggestions at *Books and Brews* the day before, and I figured I might as well try them out.

As I sketched, I thought over Ayla's offer for dating advice. Maybe I could get a couple of tips from her, even if romance wasn't in the cards for me.

I was ready for sex, and Deus was so gentle, I thought he'd be a good partner. But I didn't want to embarrass myself. The biggest challenge would be getting helpful information without revealing that I was actually a tentacled monstrosity. As long as I avoided shifting, and kept to sex in my humanesque form, it should be fine. I hoped.

My phone dinged. It was Deus. Of course it was, who else could it be?

*Study group meeting tomorrow. Join us? Coffee's on me.*

*Studying in the library tomorrow. Alone,* I typed back.

Dots rippled on the screen for several long moments. Then Deus replied, *Bianca's making cookies. Your loss. Text me if you change your mind. See you after?*

Catching my lower lip between my teeth, I nibbled at it. I could still taste him. I could still feel the silkiness of his hair between my fingers. And if I *did* have brunch with Ayla tomorrow, I could be ready for the next step…

*Deal,* I wrote, and pressed send before I could change my mind.

"Bacon," whispered a voice in my ear. "Pancakes. Fluffy scrambled eggs. French toast."

I blinked. My eyes felt sandy and my head was fuzzy. Groaning, I pushed myself into an upright position.

"Oh, you're awake," Ayla said casually, examining her red fingernails.

She was sitting on the floor, just far enough away for plausible deniability, but just near enough to lean over and whisper near my head. "I'm just sitting here, thinking about the *amazing* brunch they have in the lycan dining hall. Have you eaten there?"

"Calm your tits." I yawned, stretching my stiff muscles. "Give me a minute to get dressed and I'll come to brunch with you."

"Really?" Ayla gasped. She leaped to her feet. "Oh, my goddess! I knew we were going to be besties. Wear your tights and purple skirt."

"I don't have a purple skirt." Shuffling over to my wardrobe, I opened it and my mouth fell open.

A violet flared miniskirt hung in my closet, next to my perfectly pressed professional shirts and the little black dress I'd brought just in case.

"I borrowed it from Helena. She has a million clothes and said you can keep it if you want. It contrasts perfectly with your eyes."

I reached for my jeans.

"Stop it right there!" Ayla playfully bumped my shoulder. "Girl, we are *getting brunch*. You do not wear restrictive clothing for brunch."

She had a point. I pulled out the skirt with its stretchy material and grabbed my tights.

I WORKED up the courage to bring up the subject of sex over a stack of pancakes so tall I almost couldn't see Ayla over the top. "So… you were going to give me the sex talk?"

This was my first time eating pancakes, and I'd followed Ayla's lead, taking a fluffy pancake and smothering it in butter before covering them in maple syrup.

The lycan dining hall was built like a hunting lodge. Long, rough-hewn wooden tables were studded with faux silver candlesticks and mismatched silverware.

In one corner of the lodge, there was a pile of bean bags

where a few students lounged in their wolf forms. Ayla had stressed the importance of getting there before ten so the food wouldn't be gone. To my relief, the place was only half full, although more people were coming in by the minute.

Ayla swallowed a large bite of pancake. "I mean, sex is different for everyone, so it's sort of hard to give you specific advice. The most important things are to make sure you're ready, you're horny, and you're doing something that both of you are into. If it's your first time, maybe take it slow and don't get too kinky. The creative stuff can come later." She waved her fork at me. "Be *really* sure of what you want. Regretting sex sucks, and you don't want to start regretting it on the very first lay."

I ducked behind my towering stack of pancakes, hoping to hide my flaming cheeks. "Do you have a secret superpower that enables you to smell virgins or something?"

"No. You're just not great at being subtle. Which is kind of adorable." Ayla stuffed half a pancake in her mouth. "Most people get embarrassed talking about sex, and then they don't ask the right questions."

I took a bite of the sweet pancakes. "So, what are the right questions?"

"You have to ask yourself if this is really what you want. Will you regret being with him a year from now? Does he think your paranormal form is disgusting? And most importantly, do you have enough lube?"

The third question gave me pause.

Deus didn't know about my true form. And of course, I wasn't planning on him finding out. I'd never heard him say anything disparaging about any paranormals. It didn't seem in his nature.

Then again, Ezric seemed to always be near Deus, and the slayer had made his feelings about krakens known. I hadn't heard Deus condemn the slaughter of my kind.

"When are you thinking you'll do it?" Ayla asked, eyes twinkling. "Do we need a system? Like a sock on the door?"

"I don't know." I didn't have a clue what she was going on about, so I focused on my bacon. We didn't get many smoky things under the sea, and I found I loved its flavor. "We're keeping things casual, so I figure the time will be right at some point."

Like maybe later today.

Or never, if I lost my nerve like a skittish squid.

"Casual. Right." She narrowed her eyes. "Well, text me if you want the room to yourself."

I left brunch six pancakes and two cups of coffee fuller, and that wasn't even counting the bacon and eggs. Ayla had been right about wearing stretchy clothes.

Heading toward the library, I was in a good mood. Brunch with Ayla had been... fun. Not that I'd ever admit it to her. If the succubus suspected I'd enjoyed myself, she'd start trying to haul me to parties next.

I spent the rest of the morning looking through the library's extensive section on alchemy. The problem was, a lot of them covered the principles, which I already knew. There was a lot less on what to do if you had the basics in your head, but couldn't make them work.

*Some paranormals aren't cut out for alchemy,* Professor Farrious had said at the beginning of the term.

I'd never imagined I might be one of them. Schoolwork always came easy for me, but not this.

With a sigh, I sagged into a chair and cracked open *Alchemy for Dummies* and hoped no one I knew was in the library. I really needed to focus today.

"Wow."

My head snapped up, and I winced at the sharp twinge in my neck.

Amadeus stood over my table, surveying the mess of papers, transcriptions, and open books. "I'm going to guess your day was productive."

"Hardly." I felt like crying… and I never cried.

"Here's my attempt at amethyst." I handed him a gray rock.

Deus held it up to the light.

"Well, it sparkles," he offered after a pause. "Mind if I take a look at your transformation circle?"

"Sure. I have to clean up, anyway." I stacked the books and re-shelved them as Deus bent over my carefully drawn circle.

My head hurt, the familiar ache of a brain well used for

many hours. I looked forward to turning that brain off for a couple hours.

I took the opportunity to admire him from behind as I returned to my table. The plane of his back was straight, his muscles moving under his tight shirt as he drew something.

As I came closer, I realized he'd hastily drawn a transformation circle. The symbols had been etched out in choppy lines, and he'd swapped out a few of mine for slightly different ones.

"See." Deus pointed at my paper. "I've noticed when you write, you have this little flare, a kind of flick of your pen. I think that's messing your symbols up."

I rubbed my forehead. "Farrious says to write naturally, though."

"I know. But in your case, these little flourishes are confusing the magic. Now where's the stone?"

Deus found it on the table. "I had to make a couple of modifications, mostly for my birth sign and stuff. What you wrote should work just fine."

He placed the stone in the middle of the circle and intoned over it, "Verto permute meo potestate."

Smoke wisped over the stone before it was engulfed in flames. The fire spread lightning-fast to the edge of the paper, turning it to ash.

It flared once and died, leaving a deep-hued amethyst on the table.

I stared at it with tears of frustration burning my eyes.

It wasn't fair. I'd been trying for hours. Scratch that. I'd spent days perfecting my circles, reciting my Latin, and trying out all manner of aids.

But Deus had come in and accomplished it in five minutes.

Alarms blared. Freaking great. We'd set something on fire in the library.

"Crap. We need to go." Deus gathered my notes and shoved them into my hands.

Then he grabbed my arm and bolted. I tripped, found my footing, and ran after him through the nearest door and out onto the lawn. It was a cold October night, and goosebumps instantly erupted all over my skin.

Deus didn't stop running until we'd cleared the side of the lake and had stumbled into the woods. Most of the leaves had fallen, leaving the trees looking spindly and naked. We looked at each other in the bright moonlight and burst out laughing.

"I forgot we're not allowed to do alchemy in the library," Deus admitted, hand scrubbing across his jaw.

"Then I guess it's good I spent all afternoon failing," I said, trying to ignore the stab of disappointment that came with my admission.

Apparently, I wasn't very good at pretending I was fine.

"Seta, one C isn't a big deal." Deus put a hand on my shoulder, sending his soothing warmth spreading through me. "No one cares."

"I care," I whispered, past the lump forming in my throat. "My parents will care."

Deus leaned on a tree and pulled me against his chest. "Are your parents the overbearing type?"

"Yes, and no." I blew out a long sigh. How was I supposed to explain things to him without revealing too much?

"My mom… well, I could flunk out of Slaymore, for all she cares, as long as I come home with a mate." And as long as that mate came with allies for the Bering Clan.

I felt Deus' muscles tense, but his thumb continued rubbing soft circles on the side of my arm. "A mate, huh?"

"I don't even call home because I know she will grill me about potential mates." Taking a deep breath, I drew his smoky, calming scent into my lungs.

Deus' breathing remained steady as he listened, and somehow, I ended up pouring out far more than I'd intended to say.

"I came here to get my degree in Marine Mythology, study under Professor Mackenzie, and then use my experience here to return home to create magic-safe environments for the Bering paranormals. After that, I dreamed of spending my time studying lesser-known ocean-dwelling shifters. That's always been my plan, but my clan—er, my mom and dad—are only going to pay for undergrad. So if I want to get an advanced degree, I have to get a scholarship. And if I want a scholarship, I have to get perfect grades."

The overwhelming weight of it all closed my throat, and I slid down the tree. Deus followed me down until we were sitting half sprawled on the ground.

He was silent, gently rocking me back and forth, making

sure I knew I wasn't alone. I focused on swallowing until I was sure I could talk again without crying.

"So your parents see you as a tool to be used?" he asked at last.

"They aren't that bad. But yeah, they kind of do. Dad thinks four years is more than enough time to experience the human world and create alliances. Mom thinks a strong mate bonding could accomplish the same thing, but faster," I replied.

Dad had never been up on land at all. He hadn't even ventured out of the Deep since before I was born.

And Mom was from a long line of kraken females who'd been mated not for love, but to create alliances between clans. She was amazing, but her worth had always been tied to what she brought to her mate and clan.

We were silent for a while longer. I continued to breathe in his scent, letting it slow my pulse and ease my anxiety. The moon rose overhead, outshining the stars and scattering its light across the forest floor.

"You know who's an alchemy genius?" Deus said.

"Besides you?" I tried my best not to sound salty about it, which was a challenge. I was from the ocean, being salty was sort of my thing.

"My friend Bianca." Deus brushed his fingers through my hair.

In the moonlight, his irises were so dark they were almost purple.

I cleared my throat. "Bianca of the cookies?"

"Bianca of the cookies," he confirmed. "I bet if you

joined the study group Monday evening, she'd be happy to help with tips and tricks. What do you say?"

He meant well. But— "I study alone."

"Seta, I just don't understand. It's not shameful for other people to know things you don't and help you out. It doesn't mean you won't deserve it if you do better in Farrious' class after getting help." His teeth flashed in a luminous smile. "Besides, I want you to meet my friends. I want you to know what kind of person I am, outside of being your boy toy."

I pursed my lips. "Can you really be my boy toy if we haven't had sex yet?"

Deus raised his eyebrows, lightning flashing in his eyes. "Yet?"

# CHAPTER II
## SETA

Leaning in, our lips met in a kiss that was a sensual exploration of tongues and lips. His hand slid to my waist, pulling me onto his lap.

I adored the way my body fit against his like a puzzle piece. Grinding down gently with my hips, I elicited a groan from Deus that made me grin.

He was so incredibly *warm*, and wherever he touched me, his warmth lingered… and slowly spread downward to pool between my thighs.

Deus caressed my breast, and I arched into his palm. His tongue worked gently and insistently in my mouth, teasing, inviting. Deus' other hand slid under the waistband of my skirt and paused.

"Seta," he rumbled, voice rough. "Is this okay?"

I ground down again, feeling his length against me. "Yes."

Deus worked his fingers up to my waist and, catching the elastic of my tights, he slid them down over my hips. With the fabric out of the way, his fingers caressed the sensitive skin of my inner thigh.

His touch was driving me crazy, and without thinking, I let out a strangled moan and bit his lip.

Deus' palm traveled further up my thigh, and with each inch, I was finding it harder to breathe. I let my eyes flutter closed and leaned my forehead against his shoulder.

I gasped as his finger brushed against my core.

When his finger slipped inside, my walls contracted around him.

"I'm guessing that means it feels good?" Deus' surprise was evident in his voice.

*Not your average human clitoris,* I wanted to quip, but when his finger began to rub slowly up and down along my opening, I struggled to put together a coherent sentence.

"Good," I all but whimpered. "It's good."

Deus hauled me tighter against him, pinning his hand between our bodies. My hips bucked of their own accord, and his finger stroked me to their rhythm.

No man had ever touched me so intimately before, and it was intoxicating. It wasn't that I was a prude, I just hadn't gotten much opportunity to be around guys when I'd lived at the bottom of the sea.

As the heat built in my belly, a new desire rose to the surface.

I wanted him—all of him.

My body ached to have his bare body pressed so tightly against me that I couldn't tell where his skin ended and mine began. I threw my head back and bucked wildly against him until my legs were trembling.

"You're incredible, Seta," he said.

My core constricted, squeezing his fingers tight and causing Deus to inhale sharply. As my orgasm crested, I buried my head in his shoulder, whimpering through the pleasure threatening to wash me away.

Deus held me and stroked my hair until my shuddering stopped. "Are you all right?"

In response, I turned and kissed him, hard.

My sudden movements caused him to lose his balance, and we toppled backward into the dirt. With a wicked grin, I grabbed his wrists and pinned them next to his head.

Deus' eyes flashed and his hips gyrated against mine.

We were so doing this.

*Wait.*

We were so *not* doing this.

I wasn't going to lose my virginity on the ground, where anyone could walk by and see us, or worse, record us.

"Not here. Let's go to your place," I whispered.

Deus' aura was so brilliant I was forced to squint at him.

"Sure." His face screwed up. "Crap. Ezric's staying in my room right now. Someone flooded the bathroom in the dorm above him and his whole ceiling has to be fixed."

"Mine, then." It was a Saturday; the chances of Ayla being out were at least ninety percent.

He stroked my cheek with a thumb. "You sure?"

"I know what I want." I gave him a cocky smile and drove the point home with a little wiggle of my hips that elicited a chuckle from Deus.

Standing, I readjusted my tights, hoping I didn't look like I'd just had a romp of the sexual variety in the woods.

I turned my attention to helping Deus gather up all the papers we'd forgotten about. Several were smeared with mud and would need to be rewritten. It was worth it.

After checking my purse to make sure I still had my keycard, I took Deus' offered hand.

The few students we saw on our way back to the dormitory were dressed in fall coats and scarves to protect them against the cold. I was severely underdressed, but the warmth of Deus' aura protected me from even the sharpest gust of wind.

As we entered the dormitory, I whispered, "Could you, you know… tone it down?"

"Tone what down?" Deus' eyes flashed with mischief, even as he dimmed his aura.

We crept up to my room on the second floor. Most people were out, but music and laughter drifted down the hall from a few rooms as people opted to spend the night in with a friend or watching a film.

Unlocking my door, I peered in. The room was dark and empty.

"We're in luck." I tugged Deus into the room.

The moment the latch clicked, his hands were on me, pulling at my shirt. I helped him tug it over my head and then returned the favor, exploring his ribs and stomach with my fingers along the way.

Deus took me by the shoulders, letting his gaze wander over my exposed skin. Slowing his pace, Deus tugged one bra strap down, kissing where it met my shoulder and working his way down.

When his tongue flicked over my nipple, my legs gave out and I sat down heavily on the bed. The desire that had been simmering since my orgasm in the woods came back with the hunger of an out-of-control forest fire.

With renewed urgency, I fumbled with his belt. I could only pin him with four limbs tonight instead of all eight, but I still wanted to make the experience pleasurable for him.

His mouth stilled on my breast as my fingers danced over the silky soft boxers that covered his cock.

*Mine.*

I might not get to keep him forever, but he could be mine for the day.

The door flew open, slamming against the wall.

"Roomie, you'll never— *Ohmygoddessandvariousothergreekgodsnevermind!*" Ayla shrieked.

Heat flushed my whole body, but this time it wasn't the luxurious heat of desire... Nope. I was freaking mortified and wanted to crawl under my bed and never come out.

By the horrified look on Deus' face, he wanted the same.

"I'm leaving." Ayla covered her eyes, trying to back through the open doorway, but missed and banged into the wall. "I swear, I'm leaving."

"No," I sighed.

The sexy vibes had disappeared faster than food at a werewolf buffet.

If we tried to get back to sex now, I knew it would be awkward and strange. And as badly as I wanted Deus' body, I didn't want my first time to be awkward.

"We were just... finishing up for the night. Right, Deus?"

Deus took a deep, calming breath. His smile was regretful as he handed me my shirt. "Yeah."

"I can totally leave! It's not a problem—no worries, no questions afterward. In fact, I saw nothing." Ayla had dropped her hands, and to her credit, she kept her eyes firmly fixed on the ceiling while we dressed.

She'd probably been on the other end of objectification often enough to know what it was like.

Either she'd been out already, or was planning to go. Smokey eye makeup ringed her eyes, and her hair lay in soft waves around her face. Her blue halter top and platforms screamed *party*.

"It's okay. I'll see you tomorrow?" Deus said, buttoning my shirt for me. My heart stuttered as his fingers brushed over my collarbone.

"I'm doing my incantations paper tomorrow." I loved studying, so why did the thought of not seeing Deus the next day fill me with sadness?

"Monday, then? Study group. Bianca the genius. You'll be there?" His smile was so hopeful. What else could I possibly say?

I gave in. "Yes."

He leaned forward and brushed his lips lightly to mine. And somehow, it was the sweetest kiss he'd ever given me.

Standing, he pulled on his own shirt. "Good seeing you again, Ayla."

"Lying's bad for your skin." Ayla smirked, her tail flicking like a self-satisfied cat.

Deus shook his head and glanced back at me. "Goodnight."

The moment he'd left and closed the door behind him, Ayla threw herself back on her bed.

"What in Hades? Seta, I told you to text me if you were going to do the dirty here."

Right. She had.

"I didn't think about it," I admitted. "I only have your number in case of an emergency."

"Well, then you can't blame me for your cliterference. For the record, a *lot* of people would consider getting laid an emergency. Most of them are my cousins, but still."

She tapped a long fingernail on her chin. "How about this? Monday night, I am going to be gone until, let's say, three in the morning."

"That's ridiculous. You have class on Tuesday."

She flapped her hand. "I'll skip it."

Skipping class? I'd sooner swallow a cup full of rusty, barnacle-covered nails.

"We're not going to have sex on Monday," I insisted.

I'd have too much on my mind. Tuesday was our

alchemy mid-term, and the only thing I'd be doing late into the night was practicing my transformations.

Ayla fanned herself. "Well, it's up to you. I saw that look he gave you, and I will tell you, that man will wait for you until the end of forever."

"Maybe." I shrugged one shoulder and lay back on my pillow. "I mean, he doesn't have to. It's just casual."

Ayla lifted her head to glare at me. "Casual? Roomie, I know sex, and I know romance. I can tell you with certainty that Amadeus isn't being *casual* about any of this. I promise."

"And I'm telling *you* that we talked about it, and we agreed the whole thing is casual."

Ayla kicked her shoes off and laughed. "That guy's so into you that he's lost to the rest of space and time."

*Mine.*

I tried to hide my smile and calm the happy fluttering of my heart. "Whatever. You're my roommate—"

"Not my bestie," she parroted in my voice before bursting into giggles. "But seriously, can I tell you what went down at the party already? I'm dying to talk to someone about it, and you're the only person I know outside of the drama."

I really wanted to put my headphones in, but I also wanted to be there for my... friend.

"Sure." I pasted on a weak smile and settled on my side to listen to Ayla's rambling gossip.

"Great! So anyway, you remember Alicia? She's super

sweet, but has really bad taste in gentlemen and wanted to get drunk this weekend…"

I pressed my fingers to my mouth. My lips were puffy and still tingled from Deus' mouth. Remembering his hands running across my bare skin, I shivered. I almost regretted not telling Ayla to leave so that we could finish what we'd started.

Unfortunately, studies were more important than biological urges. I'd have to tide myself over somehow until at least Tuesday…

Deus' study group met at *All Nighter*, the 24-hour diner on campus. I arrived precisely on time, which meant no one else was there.

Freaking fintastic.

I fiddled with the end of my braid as I looked around. Linen-lined tables with red pleather booths were scattered around the space. It was already half-full and getting fuller as students got out of class for the day.

The air smelled of burned coffee and greasy fries. Maybe it wasn't too late to hide at a booth in the back and tell Deus I hadn't seen his friends. Yeah, that sounded like a great plan.

Selecting my booth, I ordered a cup of diner coffee and scowled at my notes. I was just getting in my stride when a messenger bag *thunked* heavily on the table next to me, making my coffee slosh over my notes.

I scrambled to save them from coffee stains and glared at the note-destroyer.

My blood turned to ice the moment I recognized him.

Ezric the slayer. He scooted into the booth beside me, and I pressed myself against the window to keep from touching him.

Had Deus said he'd be here? I wouldn't have agreed to come if I'd known he would be here too.

"Can I help you?" I said, in a tone that made it crystal clear I didn't plan to be of any assistance.

"Thanks for saving the table." It wasn't Ezric who answered, but a voice from behind him.

A girl with light brown skin and springy aqua hair poked her head around his shoulder. She had sparkling blue eyes, a kind smile, and spoke with a light British accent. "Sorry we're late. *Someone* was arguing with Professor Haster for almost half an hour."

"I deserved better than a D," Ezric huffed in a tone far too close to a whine for my comfort.

"Ha! I saw your paper, and no, you didn't."

This was a third speaker, a girl who was as pale as snow. Her skin didn't have one freckle, her hair and eyelashes were white.

Heck, even her pupils were white, surrounded by irises that were pale and swirled with a shade of gray. Only her mouth was a different color, a red so dark it was nearly purple.

"You must be Bianca?" I guessed.

"Yes." She cocked her head, birdlike, as she studied me. Then she slid into the booth across from me and picked up my notes. "Let's take a look at these."

"I'm Jenny," said the aqua-haired girl, sticking out a perfectly manicured hand as she scooted into the bench on the other side of Ezric. "You should try the saltwater bash. It's lovely."

I was there to study, not to eat.

"I'm not hungry." I tugged on my hair, watching Bianca as she turned a page.

We were joined by three more girls and one more guy. They all squeezed in at the table, shoving me into the corner, loudly discussing fries and chicken tenders and which flavor milkshake was best.

The group introduced themselves in a blur of names; Numina, Silvia, Tatiana and Moirus. Tatiana and Moirus kept shooting shy glances at each other, and their arms were pressed together in the booth.

"Where's Deus?" I asked, trying to make myself as small as possible to avoid being squished by the group.

Where would he sit when he did get here? We were already packed into the booth as it was. Which was a shame since I'd worn my green skirt without tights in the hopes of feeling his hand on my thigh.

"He's in class 'til three." Jenny gave me a sly, sidelong look. "Missing him, are you?"

"No!" Heat flooded my cheeks, definitely making me look guilty. "I just— I mean—"

"Leave her be. She doesn't know any of us well enough for us to start teasing her," Numina scolded.

"Seta knows me." Ezric leaned forward and winked at me.

My skin crawled, and even in my human form, I could feel my tentacles curling. He was probably the only person on the planet who could make a wink seem unfriendly.

"So she doesn't know anyone decent at this table," Numina corrected flawlessly, and I found myself liking her a little bit more.

She had the red-orange hair of a demoness, and I caught the nub of a wing poking out from her shoulder. "Deus has class until three, and he always comes over after. Though he's usually late, probably from helping snails cross the road or repairing some girl's broken nail."

"Do you remember that time he was forty-five minutes late?" Silvia snickered. Her skin had a silvery, shifting sheen, and I was pretty sure she was some sort of nymph. "He'd stopped to move tables out of the Forestry dining hall."

"He's forgiven for that one. That was the most epic party, and he only scored an invite because he helped. Ooh!" Numina clapped her hands as the waitress set her milkshake down. "Yum!"

The next few minutes were filled with the rustling of papers and the crunch of fries. I pressed my teeth together. We were supposed to be studying, but we were wasting so much time!

At least Bianca was ignoring them all and focusing on

my notes.

I leaned toward her. "So, is there anything—"

She put up a hand to stop me. "I'll tell you in a moment."

Biting my lip, I managed to stifle my sigh. I was definitely going to get a C tomorrow. *Maybe I should just give up?*

I imagined Professor Mackenzie, two years from now, as I tearfully begged him to take me under his wing for the master's program. *'I'm sorry, Seta, but your incompetence in alchemy just isn't what we're looking for in the perfect candidate...'*

Rubbing my temples, I tried to ease the building migraine.

"I think it's sweet," Tatiana gushed. I hadn't figured out what her magical deal was yet. "Deus is so nice. You know you can rely on him to help with anything."

"Yeah." Ezric rolled his eyes and stuffed three fries into his mouth.

The slayer wore a red checked lumberjack shirt today, and he popped the collar as he chewed. His eyes slid to me. "And you can rely on him to abandon you to help out with someone else's non-problem."

"Behave," Numina hissed sharply, red flickering behind her eyes. "You've ditched him plenty of times for a hookup. You can be understanding now that he's finally got a girlfriend." She smiled at me.

"We're not really putting labels on things," I muttered, but Moirus was saying something at the same time and they all turned to listen to him.

Moirus looked human, though I detected a faint whiff around him that I had always associated with the undead. He wore a black T-shirt, jeans, a small diamond stud in one ear, and kept his hair short and spiked up.

"You all hear about what happened to Fabian?" he asked.

They all burst out laughing. I didn't know what happened to Fabian, and I didn't have time to care.

Propping my head on my hand, I wished I'd ordered some fries. Then I'd have something to do, other than eavesdrop on a conversation about someone I didn't know. This was why I didn't study in groups.

No one was studying.

No one cared about alchemy.

It was just an excuse to hang out while claiming they were being responsible. Coming here had been a mistake.

I was seconds away from standing when Bianca spoke. "Okay, I think I know what you're doing wrong."

My bad mood was replaced instantly with panic. What if everything was wrong and I didn't have time to fix it?

Bianca tapped her finger on the tabletop. "So, first of all, you're starting with the wrong base symbol."

"What? Give me that." I snatched my transformation circle back.

I couldn't possibly have failed to catch such an obvious, and utterly stupid, mistake.

I traced the rune with one finger. "No I didn't."

"What's your star sign?" she asked.

"Gemini," I said.

"Birthday?"

"June 19th."

"Hm." Bianca finally looked over at the food that crowded the other end of the table. "Where's mine?" she asked.

"You didn't order any." Ezric handed her his basket. Five lonely fries sat at the bottom.

She took them and dipped them in Numina's milkshake, ignoring the other girl's protest. "You're on the cusp. I'm guessing you land on the Gemini side for astrology. You don't have any trouble with horoscopes? Star charts?"

I shook my head. Astrology wasn't that interesting to me as someone who couldn't actually see the stars from her kingdom, but I'd never had any trouble with it.

"Well, alchemy's different. You might be a Gemini in every other respect, but given that you're a sea creature, your magic might be pulling you toward the Cancer sign for this. Try it."

I wiped the rune clean with a basic incantation and bent over my paper again, feeling foolish and irritated. I should have thought of this myself.

"Too much flourish. You're going to confuse the sign." Bianca had leaned over the table to watch me. "That's the other thing. Your handwriting is lush, but it's not good for alchemy. Confuses the runes. Keep it simple."

Deus had said the same thing.

Taking a deep breath, I started over, with Bianca editorializing from the other side of the table.

As I wrote, I was surprised to discover... I sort of liked

it. Bianca was no-nonsense and eager to get her work done, like me.

Maybe I wouldn't mind a study group with her. But just her. Why did she tolerate all the others?

The others were busy teasing Moirus and Tatiana.

"Come on, tell us! Three years is ages to be together when you're young." Jenny giggled.

"I've never had a relationship that lasted more than three months," Numina volunteered.

"You just need to find a guy who's into fire and brimstone." Ezric grinned lasciviously, causing Numina to fling a fry at him.

"Our anniversary's going to be a surprise. For both of us," Moirus said firmly. Tatiana turned to him and he flushed. "I... sort of paid a witch to erase my memory. But I left myself a clue, so I know we'll figure it out together next week."

"A surprise for both of us?" Tatiana's face shone, and she leaned forward to kiss Moirus.

It looked so... comfortable.

Like it was something she did every morning and evening, and any time she felt like it in between.

Like it was something she knew she'd be doing for the rest of her life.

It seemed sort of... nice.

And I found myself longing to have the same. With Amadeus.

*No nonsense, Seta. Remember?* I gave myself a mental shake and turned my head back to my paper.

## CHAPTER 12
### SETA

"Hey." Deus appeared at the head of the table, dropping his bag.

His warm glow enveloped the table, and I instantly felt better. Jenny started to scoot out of the booth.

"What are you doing?" said Ezric.

"Letting them sit together." Jenny shot him a 'duh' look and motioned for him to do the same. "What does it look like I'm doing?"

Ezric shot me a scathing look. "No offense, Red, but I'm not moving."

An awkward silence fell over the table.

Then Deus smiled. "Don't worry about it. Thanks, Jen. Just sit back down and I'll sit on the end."

They squeezed in and I pressed myself tighter against the window.

"Sorry I'm late. Cannata ran us right up to the bell, and then Marita stopped to ask me about setting up for the fall festival next week— What's so funny?" The table had burst out laughing.

"Told you he did this," Jenny said, directing the comment toward me.

"So now that we're all here, maybe you can tell us how you two met." Silvia was looking between Deus and me, her eyes twinkling.

My cheeks heated up again. "Can't we just focus on the alchemy test?"

They laughed again... everyone except Bianca, who shot me a sympathetic look. I could definitely see myself meeting up with her to study.

"We met right outside the mansion," Deus grinned. "Seta had just pulled up. She looked lost, so I went over to help her."

I rolled my eyes. He'd made me sound like a damsel in distress. Before I could correct him, Tatiana jumped in.

"Oh my gods, that's just how Moirus and I met! At boarding school." Her eyes shone as she laid her head on his shoulder. "I'd transferred, and I had no idea where everything was. That was the first time I'd been to a fully paranormal school before... and then Moirus came up to me. And said, 'I'll take care of you.' And he has, ever since."

Moirus' hand slid around her shoulder and squeezed. "And I always will."

Bianca made a fake gagging sound, and normally I

would have agreed, but this time, I was struck with a sharp ache of longing.

They'd never be alone. These people had their lives all figured out, and everything was right on track.

Where would I be in ten years? Alone, at the bottom of the sea, helping my clan, watching over the narwhal shifters, trying to avoid my mother's matchmaking, and wondering what had happened to that gorgeous golden guy from Slaymore.

The ache was replaced by a spike of panic. I had my life figured out. I had a plan.

A plan to learn and be the best at marine mythology and go home to save the paranormals of the sea. Repopulating the Bering clan was someone else's problem. I didn't need the headache or the heartache.

"It's been really nice to study with you." I put a slight emphasis on the word *study*. "But the diner says no magic on the premises, so I'm going to go back to my room and try the transformation circle. Thanks for your help, Bianca." I met her eyes, hoping she knew that I meant it.

"No, hang on, wait," Numina pleaded as the waitress appeared to take the empty dishes. "I had a question about load-bearing runes. Like, how many do you need? Is it a formula per square inch of pressure?"

Bianca leaned over to answer her. Ezric put his head down on the table, and I was not about to scoot over him in my skirt, meaning I was stuck until he moved. Clenching my teeth, I looked down at my notes again.

Deus shot me a slightly anxious smile over Ezric's back. "Did you get some help?"

I passed over my notes. He looked at them thoughtfully for a few long moments. Then his face cleared. "Oh! You have a cusp birthday? I can't believe I didn't think about that. Did you try it out yet?"

I shook my head. "I'm not going to get kicked out of the diner like we almost got kicked out of the library."

Ezric turned his head to face me. "That sounds like an interesting story," he drawled. "Let's hear it."

"No." I started re-drawing my transformation circle, using carefully controlled and crisp penmanship. If I was stuck here, I'd be stuck doing something at least moderately useful.

"All right." Ezric sat up abruptly. I could feel his black eyes on my face, but I didn't give him the satisfaction of looking at him. "I hear you come from up near Alaska."

"Yeah." I bit my lip as I compared two runes. Was I still being too stylistic?

"That's kraken country."

My eyes jerked up to meet his before I could hide my surprise. Did I look guilty? I had nothing to look guilty about. My hand found my cuff.

I cleared my throat. "So I've heard."

He tilted his head. "Heard? Never seen one?"

"No," I lied.

"Not even a tentacle? A stirring of the waves? Maybe a weird shipwreck?"

"Bering mermaids keep to themselves," I told him,

pushing ice into my tone. "Plus, the Bering krakens may or may not exist. It's not really my problem."

"I thought you were obsessed with marine mythology? But you don't even want to look for the krakens in your own backyard?" He arched one perfect dark eyebrow, one side of his mouth turning up in a challenging smile.

It was obvious he thought I was lying about something.

Summoning an air of boredom, I rolled my shoulders and tried to look disinterested. "If there are krakens in the Bering Strait, they're down in the Deep and must keep to themselves. I don't really see our paths crossing."

"That's good. I hear they have poisoned tentacles."

We didn't. Did he already know that and was just trying to bait me into answering?

"You know, my uncle slayed a kraken." Ezric sighed, sounding almost wistful.

I forced my shoulders not to hunch up and looked down at my paper to keep him from seeing the irritation in my eyes.

Ezric continued. "He brought home a tentacle as long as our house and a handful of teeth to prove it. You know what kraken teeth go for these days?"

I unconsciously ran my tongue around my own teeth. Kraken teeth were coveted ingredients for certain spells.

Thankfully, with the advent of paranormal cooperation and the increased protection of various species, a lot of spells now had alternatives and substitutes. But some spells —usually dark ones—needed the real thing. They required actual bone, blood, and body parts.

"Uncle Jonas was one of the greats." This time, Ezric definitely sounded wistful.

Next to me, Jenny's leg was bouncing up and down. "Your Uncle Jonas was a creep who's not even allowed on Slaymore campus anymore." She flashed a dangerous smile.

Eyes widening, I stifled a gasp; her teeth had gone from a bright, even white to razor-sharp and green. *Jenny Greenteeth.*

She was part of the spirit family that lived in rivers and ponds in Great Britain. Jenny obviously had no love for monster hunters. "And if I ever see him again, I'll give him a proper thank you for taking my auntie's leg."

Ezric chuckled and spread his hands. "Look, Jen, all's fair in—"

"We're a protected species," she spat.

"Jenny's right," Numina spoke calmly. "Your uncle sucks. Most of your family does."

All humor drained from Ezric's face as it darkened. "So you all get to be proud of what you are, while I should be ashamed?"

"Nobody's saying that." Deus put a hand on Ezric's arm.

His glow radiated around the table soothingly, but Ezric jerked his arm away.

"Look, slayers are needed for plenty of things. Goddess knows my own kind are a little too fond of breaking the rules." Numina tried to play peacemaker. "You just can't go around killing indiscriminately anymore. Not any species, and definitely not a protected species."

"Well, krakens aren't protected," Ezric replied shortly. "And I'm going to bag one."

I didn't realize I was standing until Deus turned to me. "Where are you going?"

Out. Away. Anywhere but here.

Forcing a brittle smile onto my face, I rubbed my thumb against my cuff. "I'm going to go study. Alone. Or with Bianca, since she's the only one who seems to know what studying means. Move."

I said the last to Ezric, and with enough venom behind my voice that he was halfway out of the booth before he stopped to think.

"Why are you so cut up about krakens, Red?" Ezric's eyes ran down my body again, but not in his usual pervy way.

He was examining me. Could he be searching for holes in the spell that kept me human? His eyes flicked to my cuff, and I suppressed the urge to hide it behind my back.

"I'm just not interested in failing my exam." I pushed past him and stomped off.

Trying to keep from running, I slowed my step and shoved through a group of students waiting to be seated and burst through the door into the cool fall afternoon.

I didn't stop until I was halfway across the lawn.

"UGH!" I'd been so agitated, I'd forgotten to pick up my bag.

It was going to be hard to study without having all my

notes. Then again, I'd drawn my transformation circle so many times I could do it from memory... and there was no way I was going back into the diner.

Someone called my name, and I turned to see Deus jogging across the lawn. He held my bag, and his mouth was twisted in a frown. Stopping in front of me, he handed it over without a word.

I took it with a whispered thanks.

Deus took a deep breath, then stopped. "I'm sure you have your reasons, but you did seem kind of rude back there."

It was the straw that broke the kraken's tentacle.

"Rude? Rude was your best friend eulogizing his monster-killing uncle in front of Jenny," I snapped, barely resisting the urge to add 'and me.'

I'd left the 'study' session in order to get away from Ezric, and now we had to talk about him?

"Is that really why you care?" Deus asked softly.

I glared at him.

Deus shrugged. "It's just... Well, you didn't try to defend her. Heck, you didn't say anything about it. You just criticized everyone and stormed away."

Wrapping my arms around my bag, I asked the question I'd wanted to ask for some time. "Why do you hang out with him?"

Deus looked down and toed at the grass with his sneaker. His curly hair stuck out in all directions, like he'd left his dorm without brushing it, and I ignored the urge to soothe it for him.

"Ezric's... going through some stuff."

We started to walk, making a slow circuit of the saltwater lake. It was a cloudy day, and three mermaids skimmed just beneath the surface of the water, playing some sort of game with a sea urchin.

I shivered as a breeze toyed with the hem of my skirt and wished I would've worn tights. But I'd let my hormonal nonsense get the better of me.

Deus cleared his throat. "The truth is, Ezric's been disowned."

"Whoa." It was all I could say.

Maybe Ezric had just been lashing out.

Maybe he'd been saying things he didn't mean.

Deus kicked at a stone on the path. "He's always had a difficult life at home. His family summered on the island where I grew up, and I'm one of the few paranormals he was allowed to talk to. His family has old school views of who's a monster and who's not. So I was pretty much his only friend until we came to Slaymore."

Judging from the way everyone else had looked at him in the study group, Deus was likely still his only friend.

"So why'd he get disowned?" I asked.

"It's a family tradition for him to do a hunt. Slay a monster, bring back proof, get formally accepted into the family clan, get a classic weapon, all that. And the more vicious the monster, the more prestige he will get as a slayer. Except we don't have any monsters left. Everyone's protected, everyone's paranormal. Doing what his family's always done is a crime now."

I rolled my eyes. "Cry me a river. He's sad because killing people has consequences now?"

"Don't be like that. I'm not saying it's right," Deus said softly. He looked hurt, and I softened toward him momentarily. "He's sad because his family put him in an impossible situation. He can't go home until he's completed a hunt, but he can't hunt anything."

Except krakens and other unprotected species.

Another shiver skated down my spine. It was another reminder of the very real need I had to represent my people.

"Well, maybe his family's horrible and Ezric shouldn't go home." It seemed like the obvious answer to me.

Deus' hand slipped into mine. "That's exactly what I've been trying to get him to realize. His family is toxic, and he needs to stop trying to earn their respect. I'm hoping Slaymore will be good for him. It just takes kindness, exposure to good people, and time."

For a while we walked together, silent.

Maybe it would take all those things to help Ezric, but that didn't mean I had to provide them. Nor did I need to risk my safety by being around someone who still wanted to make his mommy and daddy happy... even if it meant murdering another paranormal.

And Deus could be kind without letting Ezric rant about krakens and greenteeth without challenging him. Deus had chosen not to correct Ezric in order to keep the peace. To be nice and helpful.

It might be who Amadeus was, but I didn't need a boyfriend like that.

If I were to have a boyfriend, I needed one who'd protect the krakens as fiercely as I would. The knowledge steeled my resolve to keep Amadeus as a casual fling. I couldn't let him get too close, or risk trusting him with my secrets.

That way, I wouldn't have to worry about whether he'd defend me and my kind.

And he wouldn't have to worry about standing up to his best friend and causing Ezric more hurt.

Yep. This was the best decision for both of us.

I HELD my breath as Professor Farrious handed back our exams. I was confident I'd nailed all the theory questions, but the transformation circle had accounted for half our mark… and I wasn't nearly as sure of myself on that part.

My breath whooshed out of my lungs when he finally got to me.

"Nicely done," he said, handing over my paper.

B+.

The mean little voice in the back of my head whispered, *so close*. I kept my expression neutral, despite the sting of disappointment. Receiving a B+ was good, especially in light of the not-really-a-study-session I'd attended as a last resort.

Yes, it might have been lower if not for Bianca's help and I resolved to thank her... and maybe ask her if she would be willing to have our own study group.

*Deus will be hurt by that,* the voice in the back of my mind told me.

I ignored it. We were casual. There was no reason I should make decisions based on his feelings.

Deus found me after class. Despite the fact that we were halfway through October, he wore jeans and a blue T-shirt that showed off his sun-kissed skin. He looked like he'd come straight from the beach.

Catching sight of my paper that was still face up on my desk, he gently squeezed my shoulder. "Great work. I got a B."

I twisted around to look up at him. "How? You were coaching me."

He shrugged. "I missed a couple of theory questions. So how are you feeling? Good? Great?"

"Fine." My mind was already skipping ahead to the next alchemy exam.

We had a quiz in three weeks, then nothing until finals. If I wanted an A in this class, I was going to have to get stunning marks on both exams and on all my homework.

Maybe Farrious would let me take some extra credit, just to give me a little wiggle room.

"Thought you might like to come." Deus looked at me expectantly.

Had he been talking this whole time? "Um..."

Deus cracked a smile. "You're cute when you're confused. Where did I lose you?"

"Right after asking how I was feeling," I confessed.

The hand on my shoulder slipped down my arm, leaving a tingle in its wake that traveled all the way to parts of my anatomy that had no business tingling in class. His tongue darted out over his bottom lip, and my own lips parted as I imagined his mouth on mine.

"You know what? Never mind." Deus' smile shifted and became secretive. "It'll be a surprise. Meet me at the lake tonight. Eleven."

His mouth was so hypnotizing. And the way his throat bobbed as he swallowed...

*Study plans.*

*Academic writing paper.*

*Marine mythology homework.*

So many reasons to say no...

"Sure," I murmured.

"It's a date." He kissed the back of my hand, then dropped it and made his way out of class.

## CHAPTER 13
### SETA

"I thought we were annoyed with him because he was being a douche over his friend's feelings?" Ayla was lacing up a pair of shoes made of little more than heel and string that crisscrossed perfectly around her shapely calves.

She'd been badgering me to go to the harvest festival with her, and telling her about my date was the only way to get her off my back. She'd dusted her eyes in orange and black and wore a little headband with bunny ears to accessorize her black dress.

I sighed. "He was. And now we're having a night out. And unless Ezric shows up, it won't be a problem."

"Ezric," Ayla hissed in disgust. "All right. Well, I *won't* be home tonight."

She straightened on the death-defying heels and

winked. "So enjoy your date, and anything else, and you can tell me about it tomorrow."

After she left, I touched up my makeup and wound my braid around my head like a fiery crown. I didn't want to look like I was trying too hard, so I opted for my green skirt and a dress shirt.

Finally satisfied, I headed down to the lake.

It was drizzling, but I didn't go back for an umbrella. Wet clothes were a nuisance, but I could handle a bit of water and I hated carrying an umbrella around with me.

At this hour, everyone was already in bed or at a party, so I was alone on the lawn. As I approached the lake, I saw Deus—or more accurately, I saw the boat.

The little white rowboat sat on the edge of the lake, shining with fire. As I drew closer, the fire resolved itself into at least two dozen tealights, bobbing gamely against the misty rain.

A picnic basket sat in the middle of the lights. Deus stood on the shore, under an umbrella, holding a rope to keep the boat from drifting away.

He'd exchanged his jeans and tee for black slacks and a shirt that looked remarkably like a suit. The top two buttons were open, showing off a tantalizing inch of his chest.

"You made it." His smile dazzled brighter than any candle. "I was a little afraid you'd missed what I said."

"What is all this?" I half laughed, looking at the boat.

"Well, you joined the study group on Monday even though you were uncomfortable, and it seemed to help you. I thought maybe going in the water with you might help me." He shot me a sidelong glance. "It's stupid, isn't it?"

"No, it's not stupid." I decided not to tell him that I'd hated the study session and never wanted to participate in another one. "It's…"

*Sweet. Trusting. Bold.*

I smiled. "It's nice."

"Good. Now… how do we get in?" He looked so apprehensive that I had to laugh again.

"Here, let me." I took the rope from Deus and pulled the boat in.

Once it was firmly against the bank, I guided Deus on how to climb into it. His loafers were entirely wrong for the evening's activity, but he didn't complain.

In fact, he didn't speak much at all as he got into the boat. His fingers gripped mine, tightening until I squeaked as the little rowboat rocked under him.

"Sorry," Deus gasped, grabbing hold of the side. His skin was pale, and his ever-present glow flickered.

I followed him, careful not to disturb the tealights and thinking that maybe this whole idea was nonsense. The whole thing was endearing nonsense.

"Do you know how to swim?" A new suspicion flitted across my mind as I picked up the oars.

"Not so much, no." He ran his sleeve across his glistening brow and tried to flash one of his carefree smiles.

It completely missed the mark, and was more of a grimace. "I always tried to stay away from the water in case I panicked and fried nearby swimmers. And then the anxiety about doing that just made everything worse, and... well, I've just learned to avoid swimming areas altogether."

"Right. Are you sure you're up for this?" I leaned forward and patted his thigh, trying not to notice how muscular it was beneath my palm.

Deus brushed my cheek. "Yes. I'm absolutely sure. It's important I learn to be comfortable around water."

Sitting back, I took us out on the lake with smooth strokes. The smell of salt made my skin itch. If only I could submerge...

I knocked an oar against the side and the boat rocked. Deus gasped and clutched the sides.

"It's all right," I tried to reassure him.

Deus nodded, but his throat bobbed as he gulped for air.

"I promise I won't let anything happen to you. The boat's made to rock. It won't tip over."

Not unless we did something drastic. Hades, it wouldn't even flip if we did something crazy like have sex in the boat...

My whole body flushed and my tentacles stirred inside me. Sex in the boat didn't sound like such a bad idea, as long as we got rid of the candles first. Maybe that was what Deus had been planning?

Deus' brow was still creased, and a fine sheen of sweat coated it. Maybe he *wasn't* thinking about sex in the boat.

He gestured to the dark water beneath us. "Is it anything like home for you?"

I thought of the Deep and chose my words carefully. "It's a lot colder where I live, which means we have different marine and paranormal life. But on the other side, we do have iceberg palaces for the mermaids."

"*Iceberg palaces?*" He leaned forward, and the shine in his eyes was not just the tealights.

"They—er, *we*—carve them out so that we can have air or water. We also use them to trap little pools of fish to eat fresh whenever we're hungry."

As I spoke, homesickness poured into my chest, and I found myself telling him everything I could risk telling him.

How the seagrass rippled and the eels told rude jokes, how the turtles and sharks came to us when they needed help, how the undersea currents could be used as a highway and how we played hide and seek in old wrecks.

I told him about my family, to the extent that I could. He listened while I explained my parents' struggle to run a clan that was slowly dying out, their attempt to get their children to marry outsiders and transform them to live under the sea.

"You can't do, like, a cross-agreement with some of the other mermaids?" Deus asked.

"It's complicated." That was the understatement of the century.

I described the underwater volcanoes and the imposing walls of the Deep—our home. Lit by magical jellyfish and enchanted to divert any submarines, the Deep had been our great secret for hundreds of years.

A little too secret.

"I want to turn it into a haven for endangered marine

paranormals." My excitement began to bubble over as I told him of my dreams.

"There are a lot of places on earth where paranormals can gather and hide and make a community together, but only the kra—" I cut myself off and hoped he hadn't noticed my slip. "Um, only certain clans have the space and power to make something like that under the sea."

"It sounds beautiful." Deus leaned back. He'd relaxed, little by little, and now he was no longer white-knuckling the boat. He stretched out his long legs. "I can see why you—*Crap!*"

Flame licked up the side of our picnic basket. He'd nudged a tealight a little too close to the wicker. I leaned over to cup some sea water in my hand, tipping the boat slightly to one side.

"*Ah!*" He practically threw himself in the opposite direction, causing the boat to rock violently.

Every tealight in the boat slid to one side.

"Cut it out!" I shouted, drawing in my legs to avoid the flickering flames of the candles.

Unfortunately, the more we moved, the worse the rocking got. Deus' eyes were wide with fear. He tried to move away from the candles, the boat, and the water. Causing him to clamber to one side—

It was too much.

The boat tipped further… and flipped.

Everything in the boat tumbled into the water, including Deus and me.

The fire was extinguished with a hiss. I gasped in a

shocked breath as my gills activated. Below me, I could see Deus flailing as he sank, disappearing into the gloom.

I forgot to think.

I just *wanted* him up, breathing the air again. Safe.

*Mine.*

No, he couldn't be mine forever, but he was mine for that night. Deus was only in danger because he'd tried to face his fear to make me happy.

Without waiting for my approval, my body reacted on instinct.

My legs grew longer, stretching and glowing a fiery red. Suction cups popped out along their length and my toes fused together, each tentacle ending in a long, feathered point.

Four more tentacles sprouted from my back. The salty water was perfect, like a balm on my homesick skin. Finding themselves free, my tentacles twisted joyfully as we spun down after Deus' sinking body.

Wrapping two tentacles around his waist, I drew him carefully up to the surface. His eyes were wild, his mouth open as he tried to shout but ended up choking. Why would a land-dweller try to speak while underwater?

We broke the surface seconds later, and I began pounding him on the back with a still-human arm. Deus spewed water all over my chest while he clung to me.

His heart hammered through his shirt and his shallow breath was interspersed with coughing.

"Sexy," he heaved after a couple of minutes. "I know."

"It's all right." I rubbed his back as we floated half out of the water. "I'm not going to let you go. I won't drop you."

"I know," Deus murmured.

Water streamed from his hair, which was plastered to his head. Deus' eyes seemed bluer than ever, and lightning flickered in their depths. I tried not to freeze.

"Let's get you to shore, okay?" I murmured. "Nice and easy."

But when I tried to swim, his legs tightened around me.

"I can't." His breathing was ragged.

"New plan. Let's just float. I've got you." *Unless you fry us and everything else in this lake.*

Memories of the tree he'd blackened when he'd lost control in the woods flashed through my mind. I hoped he couldn't feel my heart banging against my chest.

"Yeah." He managed a weak smile before swallowing hard and visibly trying to calm down. "We're floating really well, actually."

Then he looked down.

*Seaweed and sushi!*

My tentacles were visible.

The cuff only worked when I wanted it to, and I'd been so worried about Deus and the lake...

"You're not really a mermaid, are you?" Deus didn't sound disgusted or afraid.

He sounded... *intrigued.*

"Guilty," I admitted. "On the bright side, it makes stabilizing you in the water *really* easy."

"So..." Deus ran a finger along the sensitive, leathery skin of one tentacle.

It was the first time, other than in my imagination, that anyone had touched my shifted skin. I shivered in pleasure.

A sly smile crept across his face.

"A kraken?" he guessed. "Or is there another squid-like shifter I don't know about?"

When he ran his finger down another tentacle, I found it hard to concentrate.

"N-no," I stuttered. "I'm a kraken."

"That makes a lot of sense." His legs loosened slightly from around my waist.

"Does it?" Had I really been so bad at concealing myself?

Deus laughed. "Seta, you forget all the classic mermaid customs. You never go swimming, you never hang out with other mermaids... you don't even *know* any of the other mermaids. Most of them seem to have some kind of connection with each other."

He'd paid attention to things I hadn't thought others would notice. I didn't know what to say.

"My shoes are really heavy." Deus shifted. "And probably ruined."

"Kick them off. Your pants, too. You'll feel less constrained, and I can grab them later," I offered.

Deus raised one eyebrow. "Trying to get me naked? Do you have nefarious plans, my kraken princess?"

His fingers ghosted over my tentacles again, and he grinned wickedly at the full body tremor he caused.

Two could play that game.

I tugged on his belt until it came free and used the tips of my legs to pull his pants off. The feathered ends of my tentacle brushed over the inside of his thighs and he sucked in a harsh breath.

Using a second tentacle, I toyed with the elastic waistband of his boxers. When another spark of lightning streaked through his eyes, I came to my senses. I was playing with fire—or more accurately, lightning.

"Maybe we should go ashore," I said. "I'll help you swim there. Your first lesson."

"Seta." His voice was throaty.

With a bit of trepidation, he released his hold on me and moved his hands to the top of my shirt.

Deus undid the top button. "I'm kind of into this. I mean, if you are?"

Oh, I was definitely into it.

# CHAPTER 14
## SETA

There was something about the heat of his body being pressed against my sensitive tentacles, while the cool salty water rocked against me, that was making it hard to think clearly. My body craved him with a need stronger than even my need for water.

*Mine.*

Deus wasn't disgusted by my body, or horrified to be touched by my exploring tentacles. He hadn't run terrified into the night when he realized he was in the water with the paranormal world's monster.

With effort, I forced myself to think with my brain and not my vagina. "Deus, are you sure you won't electrocute everything if we—?"

He paused in his mission to unbutton my shirt. His legs were tangled with my tentacles, and I was enjoying exploring his muscled thighs. Our eyes met, and behind that intense blue, I saw the remnants of his fear.

"When I went under, it was all I could think about. That I was going to go off and zap you and everything else in the lake. I was so busy concentrating on it I couldn't think of anything else." He swallowed, and leaned forward until his forehead was on mine, his nose pressed to my cheek. "I was reminded that the lightning answers to me, not the other way around. I want to keep going, if you want to."

*How in control are you?* I wanted to ask, but when his hand slid between my thighs, I couldn't speak. My hips bucked, even as I tried to untangle my thoughts.

It didn't help that my tentacles had a life of their own. They'd dipped into his boxers, trembling with the desire to explore his body.

"Will you tell me?" My voice was ragged. Speaking took too much work. "If you have to... I can take you to shore..."

"I'll tell you." He pressed a kiss to my lips.

"Deus? Can I touch you?" I bit my lip, worried about his reaction. "With my tentacles?"

"You don't even need to ask." Deus had barely finished speaking before my tentacles were pulling down his boxers.

They curled around his butt, stroked his thighs, and edged closer to his stiff length. Deus groaned. Reaching beneath the water's surface, Deus found the feather tip of one tentacle and lifted it from the water.

I watched as he traced a path between the suction cups. His eyes met mine as he brought it to his lips and placed a tentative kiss on one of the cups. I whimpered, my core clenching as lust burned through me.

"So these are sensitive?" he asked, slowly moving down the tentacle to place a kiss in the middle of each.

"Goddess, yes." It felt so good it almost hurt, and I had to fight the urge to yank it from his grip.

Encouraged, Deus' tongue darted out to trace the edge of one suction cup. If I'd been an octopus, I would have inked. Wanting to return the favor, I curled the end of one tentacle around his burning erection.

Deus groaned, his hot breath blowing across my sensitive cups, even as the heat of his cock warmed my skin. His hand brushed against my throbbing core, and I longed for more of his touch. The moment he slipped two fingers inside my slit, my body suctioned greedily onto them.

When his fingers began to stroke, my tentacle slipped along his hardened length; slow, fast, then slow again. With each movement, I watched Deus' reaction, trying to learn what he liked and watching for any sign of disgust to flicker in his face. It never came.

The intimacy of being touched in my shifted form was erotic beyond my wildest dreams. I knew I should be begging him to keep my secret, or hurrying to the safety of the ocean... but all I wanted at that moment was Amadeus' touch.

"I've never felt anything this incredible. But as amazing as it is, I'm not going to last if we keep this going. Guide me where you want me to go," he whispered.

I shifted his body with my tentacles, pulling his hips

forward until our pelvises were pressed together. With no small effort, I released my hold on his fingers.

The sudden emptiness bordered on painful, and when the head of his cock bumped against my slit, the need was too much. With a flick of my hips, I shifted my position and enveloped the head of his cock.

We both stiffened. I waited for some sign that we should stop. Maybe a crackle of lightning or boom of thunder. But I saw nothing—only Deus' brilliant smile as he leaned forward to kiss me.

I rolled my hips again, taking him a tad deeper inside me. Deus groaned against my mouth. Little by little, he inched in until our hips met and he was filling me completely.

As I relaxed, growing confident in Deus' ability to control his electricity, I felt him move inside me. Even that small movement sent a surge of pleasure shooting up my spine.

"Deus," I moaned.

His hand moved back between our bodies to tease my clit. My tentacles reciprocated by winding up his legs. Deus kept it slow, working patiently as my pleasure built.

Breaking our kiss, he stared at me. "You're so beautiful."

The deep rumble of his voice was too much. I shuddered, my tight walls clenching around his cock.

"Seta, you feel amazing," Deus groaned and shifted his hips, rocking and thrusting against the greedy suction of my body.

Desire was twisting my insides in knots, and my breathing was growing ragged.

"I want—" I gasped.

He hesitated, halfway withdrawn. "Say it. Anything."

"I want more," I blurted. My tentacles twitched, pulling him in again.

"Do whatever you want to me." His skin glowed a muted gold in the black of the water. "I'm yours."

I hadn't realized simple words could be so sexy.

*Mine.*

I twined two tentacles around his waist and began to move our bodies in a halting rhythm. Once I had the hand of it, I increased the speed from an agonizingly slow but delicious pace to full on chasing the feeling multiplying inside me.

Deus let me use him to control our lovemaking. His head fell back, but his hand never moved from my clit, working his thumb in increasingly frenzied circles.

I moved faster and faster, wanting all of him inside me. My head pounded with the overwhelming desire to curl every part of myself around him and never let him go.

My body stiffened, clenching around his cock as I hit the crest of my orgasm. I cried out and my energy release caused a wave to lift us up. I clung to him with everything I had as we surged toward the edge of the lake.

Deus grabbed my waist and buried his head in my neck, his burning length thrusting into my slick core with wild abandon. "Shore. Get me to shore."

Oh. *Oh!*

No wonder he felt so hot…

I disentangled my tentacles from his legs and pushed off some nearby rocks, taking us up to where the water was too shallow to swim. He slipped out of me and I carefully deposited him on the grass.

"Seta," Deus growled my name while grabbing his cock in one hand and pumping it violently.

Hair rose on my skin, and I scrambled away, willing my tentacles back into their enchantment. His eyes locked with mine, and his muscles grew taut. A moment later, Deus roared his own release and a column of light arced from the sky.

Deus flopped back onto the scorched grass and raindrops as large as my thumbnail began to fall. He lifted his golden head to look at me and began to laugh. The sound of rumbling thunder shook the earth.

I stumbled out of the shallows on human legs and flopped down beside him. I was naked. In the middle of the lawn. And I didn't care.

Rain still pelted down around us, and I wondered if all storms at Slaymore were due to student orgasms. The ridiculous thought made me giggle.

I lay my head on Deus' bare shoulder. "Thank you."

Deus twisted his head so that he could look down at me, his expression incredulous. "I should be thanking you. Why are you thanking me?"

I said the first thing that came to mind. "Because you're sweet, kind, and let me have my first time the way I wanted it. You've been cool about the whole keeping it casual thing too."

Deus dropped his head back on the ground and cleared his throat. "Yeah."

"And you weren't weird about the tentacles," I whispered.

"Turns out I'm into them." He squeezed me briefly. "I'm into *you*. But I'm also naked in the middle of Slaymore's lawn, and I don't want to be the subject of an infamous internet video."

Oops. I shot up. "I'll get our clothes."

I went back into the water as a human. As much as I wanted to release the tentacles and feel the salt on my suckers again, I knew we'd been incredibly lucky not to have been caught.

Kicking hard, I made it down to the bottom of the lake, where I easily found Deus' shoes, belt and pants. I had to tussle briefly with a miniature kelpie over his shirt, but I won. It took a bit longer to find my shirt and skirt, since they were already half buried under silt.

I popped back to the surface and, using the rope, guided the rowboat to shore. By the time I'd finished, Deus had solved the problem of his nakedness with—

"What is that, a toga made of clouds?"

He spread his hands, showing off his work. "What do you think? Do you think it's coming back in style?"

He chuckled at my dubious expression and took the bundle of soaked clothes I held out. "One of the talents inherited from my father. Do you want one, or would you rather wear your soaking clothes?"

I opted for the wet clothes, holding my shirt closed with my hand rather than taking the time to do up all the little buttons. Together, we squelched our way across the lawn and up to the door of my dormitory.

"Seta?" Deus leaned against the wall and cupped my cheek. He ran his thumb over my lip and I couldn't help giving it a little bite. His mouth parted slightly, and his eyes got a hungry, hooded look that got that heat curling in my belly again.

I almost opened my mouth to invite him in. Ayla had said she'd be out, after all, but he went on in a rush. "Thank you for trusting me with your secret. And your body. Even if it's just a"—Deus hesitated—"fling, I'm grateful."

A pang of worry shot adrenaline through my body. "Deus, the headmistress knows what I am too, but no one else can know. You can't tell anyone."

"I know. Your secret is safe with me." He leaned in and gave me a meltingly sweet kiss.

A pang lanced through me, and for a moment, I wanted to cling to him and beg him never to let me go.

*Keep it casual, Seta. It's for the best.*

I broke away, blinking hard to keep unexpected tears at bay. With effort, I matched his soft smile. "Goodnight, Deus."

## CHAPTER 15
### SETA

"Hey."

I looked up from the fire-lighting spell I was trying to parse for basic incantations.

There stood Ezric, looking like a glorified woodsman in a green plaid shirt and jeans so tight that any *actual* woodsman would've laughed him out of the forest. His two-day stubble and his smirk suggested he'd spent a couple days with his latest fling.

"Can I help you with something?" My tone made it clear I didn't actually want to be helpful.

I wasn't happy to see him, but I was mainly irritated at the interruption. Parsing was my least favorite homework, and now that my concentration was broken, it'd take me at least fifteen minutes to get back into the zone.

"So polite, Red. I can see why Deus likes you." Ezric

fixed me with his dark eyes and flashed what he probably thought was a rakish grin. It made me want to vomit. "He said you got a good grade on the alchemy mid-term."

Clearly, Deus and I had different ideas of what constituted a good grade.

"Better than I would have gotten without Bianca's help," I admitted.

I'd already found her and thanked her, but that was none of Ezric's business.

"So. Study group works. Which brings me to my next point." He leaned over the table. "Study session, fifteen minutes, *Spellcaster's*. Let's go."

I stared at him for a moment. Did this sort of thing work for him normally? Did he go up to other random girls and say things like, *Sex, my room, fifteen minutes*?

"No thanks," I replied, looking back at my scribbled notes.

"Why not?" Ezric crossed his arms over his chest. His biceps were the size of my head, and I couldn't help but swallow as I imagined them around my throat.

Remembering what Deus had told me about Ezric's rough home-life, I debated being nice to him... but he didn't deserve it. Besides, I wasn't at Slaymore to make friends.

"Because you're a bit of a douche." I rolled my eyes. "And I prefer to study alone."

*And I don't want to spend any time in your company*, I wanted to add, but kept it to myself.

I looked back down, intending that as the end of the

conversation. Then a large hand came down over my paper, obscuring my notes. My neck snapped up to Ezric's face.

He wasn't smiling anymore. "I've known Deus for ten years. I'm his closest friend. Have you ever considered that it's in your best interest to get along with me?"

The thought had never crossed my mind, and I opened my mouth to say so, but the memory of Deus' anxious face, and what he'd said about Ezric after the last disastrous study session gave me pause.

Even if Deus and I were keeping things casual, perhaps it *was* in my best interest not to push a potential wedge between us.

And regardless of how he made my skin crawl, maybe it was best not to alienate Ezric. Besides, it would be better if he knew me as a friend before he found out what I really was…

"Anyway, Tatiana's really good at basic incantations. She comes from a long line of witches and would totally know how to do"—he waved his free hand—"Whatever it is you're doing."

I toyed with my cuff. Maybe parsing with a companion would make it more bearable. And Deus got a wounded seal-pup look every time I turned down an invitation to hang out with his friends. Imagining the happy look on Deus' face if I showed up had flying fish fluttering in my stomach.

"Fine." I gathered my notes.

At worst, it would be a couple of hours of tooth-grinding frustration, right?

Oh, how very wrong I was.

*Spellcaster's* was a witchy spot where students could have potions competitions, duels, and magic shows. They had no mochas, but they did have a large variety of mocktails, so I ordered something called a Sassy Senior while Ezric found our study table.

When I finally had my drink, I scanned the place for him —only to find him sitting alone near the door.

"Where is everyone?" I asked, still searching for the rest of the group.

Was I supposed to make polite conversation with him as we waited? Just the thought of it broke me out in a cold sweat.

Ezric poured himself something from a flask he took from his shirt pocket. "Jenny canceled because she's got a date. Tatiana and Moirus have work-study together, Silvia's in her economics elective, and Numina's got some winter solstice party committee meeting. Oh, and Deus is in class until four o'clock."

Which left him and me for fifteen minutes, plus however long it took Deus to get across campus. Had Ezric even invited him? My stomach dropped to my toes, and a chill trickled down my spine.

"You tricked me." I eyed my drink. How fast could I down it and leave?

"On the other hand, I could *really* use the help studying." He put his hands together. "Help me out and I'll put in a good word for you with Deus."

The memory of my night in the lake with Deus popped

into my mind. How much more of a good word did I actually need? Then Deus' adorable seal-pup face popped up in my mind again.

I was ahead on homework, so I could help Ezric without falling behind.

Sighing, I sagged into the seat across from him. "What do you need help with?"

Ezric's hands tightened into fists. "Marine mythology. I swear Mackenzie has it out for me. I flunked the first project, and he told me I could redo it for extra credit. So I figured, who else to go to but the marine genius herself?"

I traced an old stain on the wooden table. "Don't you have a partner to help you out?"

"She's taking the F."

This just got better and better. On the other hand, it meant I only had to talk to one person instead of two. "All right. What's your project on?"

He looked me dead in the eye. "Krakens."

The air disappeared from my lungs and my pulse leaped.

*Stay calm, Seta,* I warned myself.

Ezric was a slayer, from a family of monster hunters. It made sense that he'd want to know about the biggest monsters of the sea.

Maybe this was an opportunity to teach him we weren't the murderous beasts he thought we were. I took a deep breath and brushed my fingers over my cuff. Ezric's eyes snapped to it and I froze.

"Okay, let's get started. How about we build your

bibliography first?" I busied myself with taking out a notebook and a pen and writing *Bibliography* at the top of the page.

"Gregor's *Deep Monsters*," Ezric replied.

My pen froze as I finished the letter *B*.

*He knows,* I thought, trying to keep panic from flushing my whole body.

Slayers had improved senses, right? Could he smell my fear? Could he hear my heartbeat? I bought myself time by taking a sip of my Sassy Senior.

Ezric hadn't had any of his drink, whatever it was.

I cleared my throat. "Gregor's over two hundred years old, and his work's been disproven. Mackenzie *hates* Gregor."

Everyone with any common sense did. Gregor had sailed the Deep with the aim of putting any paranormal head he could find on his castle wall.

"Mackenzie also said that he doesn't take off marks for opposing viewpoints." Ezric pinned me with his eyes and I fought the urge to squirm.

"He takes points off for bad sources." My mind raced, and I wanted to touch my cuff, to reassure myself that my tentacles were safe and hidden.

Ezric continued to study me, a single brow raised in challenge.

"I don't actually think Gregor's a… bad idea." I had to concentrate to keep my lip from curling. "But you will need to contrast him with more modern sources."

I finished writing *Bibliography*, took a deep breath, and

forced my hand to write *Gregor* in the first slot. It felt like I'd become a traitor to my own kind.

"Easy. Gregor's the only one who reported on a kraken's poison whip. That's one slide right there—as well as a slide on why no one else reported it."

I wanted to whip him with something of my own.

"Maybe because krakens don't have a poison whip?" I suggested through gritted teeth, suddenly wishing I did possess a whip.

"And how do you know? Do you have a kraken bestie? Or did you travel the oceans with Gregor a couple hundred years ago?"

I clenched my fist under the table until my nails bit into my palm. "Maybe you *should* make a slide on that. On how Gregor made one claim that at least twenty other books deny."

He leaned forward, a strange glint in his eye. "Twenty books that had an agenda. Of *course* you're going to downplay how dangerous a monster is since you are determined to give it protected status. I bet you'll lie about how boats go missing in kraken territory, too. And what about how many have disappeared off the coast of Alaska in the last year?"

"Those were poachers, and they deserved what they got," I snarled.

"Yeah? What did they get?"

Too late I realized what that gleam in his eye was. It was cunning. He'd been drawing a trap around me, and I was two steps from admitting exactly what I was to him.

Sitting back in my seat, I chose my words carefully. "The guardians of the Deep broke the boats, but left the men alive. They sang incantations of healing for the injured whales, and my clan took the men to the nearest island. They were then picked up by their human government and dealt with."

His black eyes bore into me. For a long time, neither of us spoke. Then he reached under the table and drew something from the pocket of his jeans. "Gentle giants? Is that what your 'guardians of the Deep' are? Then what are these for?"

He held up a triangular tooth the size of his palm. One edge was serrated. The root was covered in a dry brown substance. Blood.

His uncle's war trophy. One of my brethren had been slain in cold blood, so that Ezric's murderous Uncle Jonas could bring home trinkets and bragging rights. And now Ezric was waving it in my face.

My whole body went stiff, even as my beast stirred inside me.

Either Ezric didn't notice the change in my demeanor, or he didn't care. Holding the tooth up, he tilted it this way and that.

His voice was mockingly curious as he asked, "How many people do you think this tooth bit down on? How many lives were destroyed by one thing?"

"Put that away." My voice was so cold I was surprised my breath didn't frost over.

"Why? Because it doesn't fit with your narrative of a

gentle giant?" He brandished the tooth. "This was meant to pierce bone and tear meat. No creature on this earth has teeth like this. Except for *dragons*." The way he said it told me what he thought of them and their protected status.

This was a mistake, and Deus was sadly mistaken about his friend. Ezric wasn't about to change his mind about krakens, or about me. And I didn't want anything to do with him.

Gathering my things, I stood up. "Thanks for the waste of time. The next time you feel like having a study session, don't bother asking me."

He got to his feet. "Look, Seta. I don't want us to be enemies."

"I don't believe you, Ezric. You seem to love trying to upset me."

"Aw, Seta. Just one more thing before you go." Ezric's black eyes met mine. They were cold and filled with cruelty.

His hand darted out, too fast for me to really see, grabbing the full glass he'd poured for himself. With a string of shouted Latin, he tossed the contents of the glass all over me.

A prickling fire flashed over my body, like all my limbs had gone to sleep and were waking up at the same time. The prickle faded, first from my right leg, then my right arm.

The spell seemed to be flowing over my body, moving toward my left wrist. My cuff glowed a bright blue as it sucked up the spell and I was left wet and seething with rage.

I wasn't an expert with magic, but it felt like some kind of revelation spell. Under normal circumstances, it would have released my tentacles, but the cuff had protected me from it.

Of course, mermaids didn't have a reason to use enchanted objects to hide their fins and tails. So just by defying Ezric's spell, I'd given him more proof that I wasn't what I claimed to be.

And he knew it.

Ezric set the glass on the table with a calculated thump.

"What's wrong, little mermaid?" he cooed softly.

My heart raced as his hand curled into a fist. What other weapons, spells or enchantments was he hiding? A spear gun? A magical trident or harpoon?

His hand moved again, and I didn't wait to find out.

I grabbed the edge of the table, lifted it, and shoved, putting the full force of my kraken body behind it. The table flew into Ezric, knocking him against the wall. His head *thunked* on the plaster and he slid to the floor.

For a moment, he was terribly still. Then he blinked dazedly.

The whole café was quiet. I was suddenly aware of dozens of eyes darting between me, the table, and Ezric.

How long had they been watching us? What did they know? Did *everyone* realize I wasn't a mermaid?

My breath came in shallow gasps. I had to get out of there. But just as I turned to flee, the one person I wanted to see least walked in.

Deus' smile froze on his face as he saw me. Then he

looked at the mess, and at Ezric, shoving the table off his legs and his smile faded. "What's going on?"

"Your girlfriend's a crazy monster. That's what's going on," spat Ezric, pushing himself up off the floor.

There was so much I wanted to say, but no words would come.

Deus didn't look at me as he went over and righted the table. He didn't offer to help Ezric stand, but he also didn't ask why I was soaking wet.

Tears blurred my vision as my heart shattered. Not wanting to make more of a spectacle of myself, I shoved past them, making my way through the door and out into the chill afternoon.

I needed to harden my heart. Deus wasn't my boyfriend... and he couldn't ever be anything more than a casual fling if he wouldn't defend me from someone who called me a crazy monster. Even if that someone was his best friend.

Heck, as much as he'd seemed to like it in the lake, maybe Deus thought I was a monster.

It didn't matter. None of it mattered. I should have spent the day studying by myself. I shouldn't have tried to build friendships or do things just to make Deus happy. I'd given in to the nonsense and had ended up scared and heartbroken. Lesson learned.

"Seta, wait! Surely you can stop to talk for five minutes." Deus jogged up beside me.

Reaching out, he grabbed my arm to bring me to a gentle stop. In that moment, I both despised and loathed the familiar, comforting warmth that spread through me at his touch.

Turning toward him, I held my bag in front of me like a shield to protect my breaking heart.

"*No.*" The single word left my lips with such force, Deus froze as though in a spell. "I *literally* tried to make nice with Ezric and help with his project even after he tricked me into going with him to Spellcaster's... and all because I wanted to make you happy!"

I took a deep breath and straightened my spine. "Just like always, he proved to be an arrogant arse who takes delight in being cruel. There's no way I'm wasting another precious second of my life in his presence. He doesn't respect me, so I don't have to respect him. And if you can't respect my decision, then this thing between us isn't going to work."

"Seta." Deus reached for me and I stumbled back.

People were starting to look at us, and heat seared across my face.

Deus dropped his hands and lowered his voice. "You can't ask me to choose between you and my best friend."

"You're right." I choked back a sob, not wanting to let him see me cry.

I couldn't ask that of him. But I could remove myself from the situation.

Fighting to keep my voice steady as tears welled behind my eyes, I whispered, "Well, you don't need a monster for a girlfriend, anyway."

Without waiting for a response, I turned and fled before my strong façade broke down.

I ran across the lawn, keeping my head tucked. No one needed to see my shame. If I could just get back to my room without crying, I'd be fine. I could waste the rest of my lunch, then get back on track for the next session—

Footsteps pounded on the grass behind me. "Stop!"

I sped up.

"Seta, *stop*." Deus' legs were a lot longer than mine, and he'd been on land his whole life. He caught up to me easily.

I jerked away from him, using my hair as a curtain to hide.

"Monster? How can you say that about yourself?"

"Me?" I spun to face him, and despite my best efforts, my tears began to fall. "Ezric said them first. Back in *Spellcaster's*. It's okay for him to say it, but not for me?"

Deus reached to brush the tears from my cheeks, then pulled back. "Of course it was wrong for Ezric to say it. But is it right for me to lose a friendship for a girlfriend I don't even have?"

My stomach twisted. "What does that mean?"

Deus snorted and ran a hand through his curls. His smile lacked humor and warmth. "Come on, Seta. You never wanted to be mine, and you never let me forget it."

I opened my mouth to fling back a reply. But nothing came. Deus was right. There'd been signs he'd wanted more, but I'd never allowed him to be my boyfriend.

I'd never allowed *myself* to be his girlfriend. I'd been

blinded by my own goals and my determination not to fall into the role my parents wanted by finding a mate.

Why hadn't I put the same amount of effort into building a relationship with Deus as I had in fighting against that happening? Goddess, I was so stupid.

"Ezric has been dealt a rough hand and I'm not going to trade a real friendship for a relationship I'm never going to get. I'm sorry if that bothers you." Deus's glow was gone, and sadness was the only thing that radiated from him. "Maybe we can work something else out."

I hugged my bag tighter to my chest, clinging to it as though it were a life-preserver in the middle of a tumultuous sea. "Not everything works out, Deus. Because you can't make everyone happy all the time, especially with Ezric lurking around. You know Ezric's a jerk, but you're too busy trying to help him be happy to think about what it's going to cost you."

"Yeah. The woman who only wants me for sex." Deus' eyes widened and his hand went up to his mouth.

His words pierced my heart like an arrow, and I swallowed hard to clear the lump from my throat. "I'm talking about your other friends, Deus. All of them. Jenny, Bianca, and Moirus—everyone who likes hanging out with you! None of them like him. And one day, they'll decide that as much as they enjoy hanging out with you, it isn't worth spending their time tolerating him."

"You know he has issues—"

"We all do. Maybe *he* should spend some time actually working on them," I snapped.

A couple of passing students craned their heads, but I was past caring. "Maybe he was worth being friends with once. Maybe there was a time when he could have turned away from his family. But no matter how nice you are to him, you can't change his opinions if he doesn't want to change. I hope you figure that out before you lose everything."

Deus' mouth moved like a fish. From across the lawn, Ezric yelled, "Leave it, man! She's not worth it."

I blinked furiously, my tears streaming down to my chin.

"He's right. I'm not worth it. Just leave me alone, Deus," I said softly, and left before I could embarrass either of us any further.

I didn't stop until I got back to my dorm room. Then I flung myself down on my bed, curled into a ball, and let my emotions loose for the first time in years.

# CHAPTER 16
## AMADEUS

"He's right. I'm not worth it. Just leave me alone, Deus." She turned and hurried away before I could speak.

My world began to crumble around me as I watched her hurrying across the lawn. I couldn't let her go. It was time to lay everything on the line.

As I moved to follow her, a heavy hand landed on my shoulder. "Come on, bro. Let's get you a drink."

I shrugged his hand off my shoulder. "This isn't the time."

"I know it doesn't seem like it, but this is a good thing. She's not what she seems." Ezric's voice was too loud, and the students scattered around the lawn were still watching the unfolding drama with interest.

My soul screamed for me to chase after Seta, but I

needed to take care of something first... and out in the open wasn't the place to do it. Turning on my heel, I strode off toward my dorm room with Ezric jogging to keep up.

Neither of us spoke until I unlocked the door to my room. Then Ezric wasted no time.

"Deus, surely you aren't mad over being dumped by that loser? She's not a mermaid, she's a freaking monster—"

I doubted Ezric even saw my fist coming. It connected with his face with enough force to send Ezric flying back against the closed door. The dishes in the cabinet rattled, and a picture frame hanging in the entryway crashed to the ground.

"I'm proud of you, De." Ezric used his thumb to swipe the blood from his busted lip. "I didn't think you had a violent bone in your body."

I ran a trembling hand through my hair. Ezric's sharp gaze studied my hand, probably believing it was a sign of weakness. Little did the slayer know it was taking every ounce of self-control I possessed to keep my powers tightly leashed so I didn't light him up like the Fourth of July.

"Get your stuff and leave. You have thirty minutes," I snarled, moving away from the entryway and into the living room.

"You can't be serious." Ezric stormed after me. "Does she have you whipped already? She's a kraken! Do you understand what that means?"

"What Seta is, or is not, is none of your business." I ground my teeth together, teetering on the edge of losing control.

Ezric collapsed into the chair across from me, shock etched across his features. "You've been my friend for years and you know better than anyone the pain my family has put me through. Which means you know exactly why a kraken on campus is my business. You know what this will mean for me!"

It was my turn to be shocked. "You can't be serious. The only monsters in this whole situation are your parents."

"Maybe they are right, Deus. Maybe there is no other way to truly be ready to be a slayer until you've faced down a literal nightmare." Ezric held out his hands, pleading with me to understand.

Icy horror seeped through my bones. I'd always wanted to see the best in Ezric, and I'd never judged him by the actions of his family. But I was seeing my childhood best friend in a different light, and it wasn't an attractive look.

"I'd suspected Seta wasn't a mer for a while, and I almost proved it today with an advanced spell. It would have worked if it hadn't been for that cuff she was wearing. She's using it to keep her form hidden." Ezric pressed his fingers to the swollen side of his face. "A kraken has been under my nose this whole time."

If she was a kraken and they are truly the monsters your family claims them to be, then why hasn't she slaughtered half the campus? You're judging her unfairly." I pointed out, my tone dripping with disgust.

Ezric snorted and lifted a shoulder in a dismissive shrug. "There are ways around that. Like today in *Spellcaster's*. It looked like I spilled a drink and then she lost it and attacked me. If she'd shifted to her true form when attacking me, I would have had every right to defend myself. A kraken is a beast. They aren't like us."

"Get out. Now." I rose to my feet, every hair on my body lifting as electricity hummed in the air. "And if you ever think of laying a finger on Seta, or any other paranormal species whether they are protected or not, know that I will come for you with the full weight of my power behind me."

"Are you serious right now?" Ezric leaped to his feet. "Is she so good in bed that you'd threaten me? I'm a slayer. You don't want me as an enemy, Amadeus."

I focused on my breathing, trying to ground my lightning even as the building shook from the thunderous crashes outside. Ezric should have realized the danger he was in, but he ignored it and stepped forward until we were nearly nose to nose.

"What makes her so special, Deus? Don't tell me you have a tentacle kink." Ezric's lip curled in disgust. "Every female on campus would happily throw herself on your cock, but you want to defile yourself by screwing a monster?"

How dare he turn something beautiful I shared with Seta into something vile? I'd seen the fear and trepidation in her face at the lake after her shift. She'd expected me to be grossed out, or terrified, of her body.

The fact that she thought those would be normal reactions broke my heart. She was beautiful, regardless of her form, and I hated that history had taught krakens that they wouldn't be accepted.

Not to mention that night at the lake with her tentacles touching and exploring every part of my body... while her tight walls sucked my cock as though she was simultaneously giving me a blowjob... it had been the most intoxicating experience of my life. And one I prayed I'd get to experience again.

My fists never touched Ezric.

They didn't have to.

Lightning leaped from my body and surged into his. I'd heard being tazed was a painful experience, but this looked far worse. Ezric's muscles seized and his eyes rolled back into his skull. The acrid scent of smoke filled the dorm, causing me to cough.

Reigning in my powers, I watched Ezric's body collapse to the ground. With my heightened senses, I could still pick up the steady sound of his heartbeat. I hadn't killed him. Which was good. I guess.

Grabbing his legs, I dragged him out of the dorm and into the hallway. Returning inside, I packed his duffle bag with all his stuff and tossed it onto his unconscious body in the hall.

Task finished, I headed inside and locked the door.

I wanted to rush to Seta's side and beg her for another chance. It was time I told her about my suspicions that she was my mate, even if it should be impossible. I wanted to hold her and soothe my soul with the knowledge she was safe.

Her sorrow was pulling at my soul, even from across campus.

But my legs gave out, and I sagged to the floor.

The confrontation with Ezric had taken its toll on my body. Restraining the wild power of lightning was dangerous. Just as it could torch a tree or person, keeping it trapped inside caused it to burn through my energy reserves.

I tried to push myself off the floor. Seta was probably crying, believing I'd taken Ezric's side. She was hurting, and it was my fault.

My arms gave out, and I collapsed onto the singed hardwood floor. Despite my best efforts, my eyelids grew heavy and my muscles went slack.

*Please don't hate me, Seta.*

Everything went black.

# CHAPTER 17
## SETA

I cried myself to sleep and woke the next morning with a pounding headache. Something was buzzing just over the side of the bed.

It stopped, only to start again a moment later. I tried to ignore it in favor of feeling sorry for myself, but the sound grew increasingly annoying.

Flinging my arm out, I felt around in my bag until I found the offender—my phone. It only buzzed for alarms and phone calls, and I only ever got phone calls from one person. And I definitely wasn't in the mood to talk to him.

But to my surprise, it was Ayla's number on the screen. I'd also missed seven calls from her.

Tapping the screen to answer the call, I asked, "What?"

"Seta, *where are you*? Are you okay? Did you get

kidnapped? Has someone left you for dead? Give me visual clues and I'll help figure out where you're being held."

I sniffed. "Gray ceiling, gray bed, gray wardrobe, gray desk. I'm in our room."

There was a long pause on the other end of the line.

"Are you, like… tied down?" Ayla whispered.

"No."

This time the pause lasted so long I thought maybe she'd hung up.

"So you missed class by choice?" Ayla sounded incredulous.

I took the phone away from my ear and squinted at the time. Crap! I was supposed to be in beginner's incantations. If I ran now, I could make it for the last half hour—

Screw it. I didn't feel like running anywhere, and I had such high grades in that class I could flunk the final and still get an A. "It's just a review."

More silence.

When Ayla spoke again, her voice was frosty instead of worried. "All right. Who are you, and why do you have my friend's phone?"

"Ayla, it's me. I'm fine. Also, I'm not sure we are even friends," I replied dully.

"Well played, roomie. See you in a minute." Ayla hung up.

I frowned at the phone before setting it on the nightstand. She had class for another thirty-five minutes at least, so how would she see me in a minute?

But my questions were answered when the succubus

breezed through the door twenty minutes later. She carried two to-go cups of hot chocolate and a paper bag.

Kicking off her kitten heels, she sat on her bed and leaned over to hand me one of the hot chocolates. "Okay, what's the deal?"

Easing into a sitting position, I took a sip of hot chocolate. It was velvety on my tongue and spread warmth through me.

"I'm fine." I would be, anyway.

Today I could hide in my room, but tomorrow I had to be back on track. I had alchemy class the next day, and it was the one review I couldn't miss.

"Seta, you are not fine. You haven't missed a single minute of a single class. Hades, I bet you could have tentacle rot and you'd still show up for class. Wait. Is tentacle rot even a thing? Is that what's wrong with you?"

"Wh... What are you talking about?" My belly flopped unpleasantly, and suddenly the hot chocolate tasted bitter on my tongue.

Ayla ignored my question. "Did... Deus hurt you? Do I have someone to kill?"

"No, he didn't, not really. I don't want to talk about it—"

"I am your friend," she hissed, cutting me off. Her eyes blazed so brightly they changed color. *I didn't even know a succubus could do that,* I thought. They were mesmerizing.

"People care about you, whether you want us to or not. Being alone with your problems won't fix them. Ugh. Are all krakens so obstinate?"

She scooted back on her bed and fished around in her

bag until she found a bar of chocolate, which she tossed at me. "Isn't this, like, why you're all dying out? Because you're all loners and can't find someone to screw?"

I was too busy staring at her open-mouthed to catch the chocolate, and one corner of it hit me in the chest.

"How did you know?" I blurted.

Ayla took a long drink of hot chocolate, eyeing me over the rim. "Seta, you are so very clearly not a mermaid. You don't do the hair flip, you don't hang out in the lake, you don't care about shells unless you're trying to figure out what's inside them, and you never spend time socializing with actual mermaids. And once when you came out of the bathroom I caught a glimpse of tentacle."

I sat slack-jawed as she spoke. How could I have been so careless? My cuff must have been loose and because I'd been relaxed after a shower, I'd forgotten to keep a tight grip on my form.

"Look, I don't care. You're tidy, you clean the sink, you don't party so much that you puke all over our room, and aside from that one time, you keep your sexy times to yourself. You're a good roommate. And you *could* be a good friend... if you'd let people in. We could build our own clan by supporting each other."

Ayla knew what I was, and instead of being afraid, she'd continued to stay in the room with me. And as much as she loved gossip, she'd kept my secret.

I loved the ocean, but the Deep was horribly lonely. I'd been focused on trying to gain the tools to give myself a purpose and make myself happier once I returned to the abyss, but in doing so, I'd missed out on giving myself the chance to build a life without heartbreaking loneliness.

While I didn't want to be forced into a loveless mating just to help repopulate my kind, my resolve to help my clan and the rest of the krakens hadn't wavered. But did I actually need to return to the Deep to assist my people?

Who knew? Maybe it would be more beneficial if I stayed on land.

But if I were going to try to build a life outside of those I knew in the sea, I'd need to open my heart to those on land. I'd need to take a chance on friends... and maybe even give myself the chance to be open to being loved.

Determined to make up for lost time, I whispered weakly, "Thanks for the hot chocolate... and for being my friend."

Ayla beamed, then her face grew serious. "You're welcome. Now what's going on? There's heartbreak written all over your aura."

I needed a friend. It was time I opened up to someone.

Taking a steadying breath, I tried to present the facts in an academic way, but Ayla kept butting in, asking for details about one thing or another. The more I talked about Ezric, the darker her expression grew.

"Do you think we can prove he's out to get you? Discrimination can get a student expelled here. Life with so many different paranormals is delicate enough; for one to be openly against another species is actually dangerous."

"The problem is, I'm officially unofficial." I grimaced. "No one's supposed to know I'm a kraken. Headmistress

Losia said some people would react like this, so it was better to hide my true nature until I was here long enough to prove krakens could live peaceably with others without hurting them."

"Well, hopefully that means Ezric can't make a move against you. If everyone thought he was attacking a mermaid, he'd be expelled."

Which meant I'd have to put up with him for another three and a half years.

*Wonderful.*

The floor right outside our door creaked, and both our heads snapped toward the door.

"Don't even think about coming in," Ayla growled, mouthing the word *Amadeus* at me.

My lungs constricted, and my whole body flushed with panic. I was supposed to be tough, not caring about friends or relationships.... he couldn't see me openly weeping and pathetic.

There was a short pause before Deus spoke from the other side of the door. "You know what? I *am* thinking about coming in. And if I can't come in, I'll say what I have to say out here, and everyone can hear it."

Deus sounded defiant, but his voice shook a little, as though he wasn't used to standing up for what he wanted.

Ayla brandished her empty hot chocolate cup and whispered far too loudly. "Watch out, looks like the golden boy might be growing a spine."

I sighed. "You can come in, Deus."

Ayla shot me a look.

"I don't need him airing our dirty laundry for the whole hall to hear," I muttered.

"Well, I'm staying here." Ayla got up and put her hands on her hips. "I've got your back, bestie."

I couldn't help but roll my eyes. I'd just opened my heart to her as a friend, and she'd already decided we were best friends. Give an inch, and Ayla would take a mile.

Deus let himself in and my fingers clutched my throat at the sight of his pale, gray skin. He wasn't glowing, not even a little. Without that magic, his skin had become more lackluster than that of a mortal. His eyes, though, were so blue it hurt to look at them.

I wished I could disappear into the depths of the sea, and for a moment, I considered diving under my blanket. But it was time to face Deus.

It was time to be open about my feelings.

*All* of them.

Deus stared at me, then the corner of his mouth quirked up in the tiniest of smiles. "I liked talking back to you. It felt good."

I blinked, and even Deus looked a little surprised at himself. Maybe it wasn't too late for him to learn to say no and stand up for what he wanted after all.

Ayla was less than impressed and glared at Deus, her eyes glowing. "That's your opening line, Casanova?"

"Seta, I hate confrontation. I hate making people mad, but I love making people happy. Yesterday was hard because I was between two people I cared about and I just wanted to smooth things out." Deus put his hand on the back of his neck. "I watched you leave and wanted to tell you to come back. I wanted to take you back to my place and wait until the argument blew over. But I realized I can't do that all the time, nor can I 'nice' my way into creating a perfect world. I have to say no sometimes. Yesterday, I said no to Ezric." Deus swallowed hard and met my eyes. "And today I have to say no to you."

He was supposed to be mine.

I knew it was true, even though I'd been adamant in denying it.

A yawning emptiness opened in the pit of my belly, threatening to drag me down. I wanted to scream from the pain, but no sound came out. A fresh wave of tears threatened to break to the surface, and I let them come.

I'd decided to let those I cared about in... to let them see the real me. So I let Deus see me as I was. Crying silently, I stared unseeing at my blanket as I waited for him to leave.

"No, Seta. I don't want to be your casual fling. And no, I don't want to avoid labels. I want to be your boyfriend... and more. You don't have to say yes to me, but if you only want sex, you're going to have to find it with someone else."

My eyes met his, struggling to understand. Was he breaking up with me, or trying to keep me?

A golden shimmer ran over his skin. "I want to walk you home from class and tuck you into bed. I want to take you on midnight boat rides and swims. I want to build clouds for you and have a real picnic on the lawn. I want you to read my favorite books and listen to my favorite songs. I want to fall asleep on the couch with you in my arms... without having any sex at all—" Deus paused. "I'm sorry, I'm making you uncomfortable."

The last was said to Ayla, whose expression had gone from murderous to gleeful.

"You are definitely *not*," she said, pressing her hands together and shifting her weight from foot to foot.

I knew her well enough to know she was barely containing her excitement.

"I guess I'm finished anyway." He looked back at me, his eyes blazing in a way that made my skin burn. "I always thought that helping people would help the whole world. Now I realize by doing that, I'm exhausting myself. It's time I stop failing the one person who truly matters to me. That's you, Seta. If you'll let me."

*Yes,* my heart quivered.

But there was something I needed to know first. "What about Ezric?"

Lightning crackled through Deus' eyes. "He tried to tell me what you were, but I made it clear I didn't care. I told him he shouldn't care, either. Ezric wasn't happy when I told him to get his stuff and get out. I think we both saw a different side of each other, and even if you don't want to be together, I can't be his friend until he shows he truly wants to change. I can't save him if he doesn't want to be saved."

His glow had grown stronger as his voice became more determined. Now he leaned against the door, the nervousness replaced by a confident sense of resolve.

My broken heart began to weave itself back together.

Deus had just given up his friendship with Ezric, a childhood friend, with no guarantee that he'd end up with me. And he was willing to walk away from me if I couldn't accept his terms.

*Mine.*

I wasn't willing to walk away from him.

Not today, not next year, not *ever*.

"Yes." Jumping from the bed, I threw myself into his arms.

Deus held me for several minutes without speaking. "Seta, may I make you brunch? To apologize for being an idiot?"

I looked at Ayla. She threw her hands in the air. "I've been waiting for you to kiss him for five minutes. Go! Have a good time. *And text me* if you bring him home this time, okay?"

"No need. If Seta forgives me, my dorm room is empty." Deus winked down at me.

"Get your cute butt out of here." Kissing Deus on the cheek, I gently pushed him out the door. "Come back in thirty minutes and I'll be ready."

I watched him walk down the hall.

*He really did have a great butt.*

# CHAPTER 18
## SETA

Deus showed back up exactly thirty minutes later, and Ayla practically shoved me into his arms.

We walked out into the brilliant late morning sunshine. Deus kept his arm around me as he led me to his dormitory building.

When he opened the door, I realized that as much as Ayla was growing on me, I was low-key jealous of Deus' dorm room. He had a bed, a bath, a table, and a kitchenette all to himself.

His bed was hidden behind a bookcase stuffed with vases, photos, and even a few textbooks. The walls were hung with pictures of the Greek island he'd called home for most of his life, as well as photos of sun-kissed, stunning people. He caught me staring at them.

"Those are my family members. I have, like, forty half-siblings. Honestly, it's exhausting." He ducked into his mini fridge. "My dad is the worst, though."

"Probably not worse than Ezric's dad," I pointed out.

I regretted the snide remark immediately, but Deus laughed. "You're right. My dad never disowned me or told me to risk certain death before I could become a real member of the family. It does put things into perspective."

Deus pulled a bowl from the fridge and poured its contents into a nonstick pan. "Marinated filet of salmon. Ready in…"

He splayed his hand six inches above the pan and concentrated. A few seconds later, two miniature lightning bolts hit the fish, searing the sauce and blackening the surface. The smell of cooked fish, burned garlic and miso filled the air.

"It's ready now," he said with a flourish, and grabbed two plates from the cabinet.

The fish was overcooked, but I didn't say anything. As a kraken, I was used to eating my food raw. One of my first land etiquette rules had been how to eat what land-dwellers ate. And even if I was inexperienced at dating, I knew enough not to criticize his cooking.

"I need to tell you something," Deus said as I dipped my spoon in the miso sauce.

It was delicious, and I hummed in appreciation. "Go ahead, I'm listening."

"I think you might be my fated mate," Deus blurted.

I almost dropped my spoon.

"*What?*" I asked, my voice hitting a note that could crack glass.

Deus laughed nervously. "From the moment I saw you pull up to Slaymore, I've been drawn to you like lightning to metal. I can feel your heightened emotions even when we aren't near each other. And I feel lost when I'm not around you."

*Mine.*

Could he be right? I'd been so worried about being forced to take a mate, I hadn't ever considered the possibility that I might meet a fated mate. I'd never heard of a kraken finding a mate, but maybe our mates weren't in the sea?

I knew that was the moment where I should tell him what I felt, but my body was frozen. Yesterday, I'd refused to consider him as more than a fling. Was I ready to make the massive leap to being mates? Even if we were fated mates?

"You don't have to say anything. I know there is still so much we need to learn about each other, but I wanted to be clear about what I feel for you." Deus reached out to cup my face in his warm palm. "We can take things slow, but you are the only one for me. And I'm willing to wait until you feel the same. For now, I want to learn about you."

"What do you want to know?" I croaked, my mind still struggling to process his confession.

"Everything." Deus' serious expression caused my stomach to flop like a fish out of water.

Goddess! Why did he have to be so sweet?

After brunch, he gave me the grand tour of his place, and pointed out each of his brothers and cousins by name... all of which I promptly forgot. He had more family members than there were krakens in the entire sea, and they were all breathtakingly beautiful... like gods and goddesses.

"So this is why you're not more arrogant about your looks," I joked. "Your whole family is drop-dead gorgeous."

"Right? I'm basically the ugly duckling." He traced the damaged corner of a picture frame hanging in the entryway.

"You're beautiful," I replied without thinking.

Deus' smile was so radiant, my breath caught in my chest. "Thanks. That means a lot from you."

He pulled me into his arms and our mouths met. Deus tasted salty as the ocean thanks to the seafood brunch... which might be gross to another girl, but to a kraken, it was wonderful.

Grabbing his shirt, I pulled his hard body against me. The force knocked us into the wall, causing the picture frames to rattle and bounce precariously. He caught one as it fell from its nail.

He broke away, face flushed and eyes sizzling with desire. "Not to brag, but my bed is pretty interesting."

I snorted. "Does Slaymore have a *Pickup Lines 101* course? Because you should consider attending it."

"Ha-ha." He picked me up, and I wrapped my legs around his waist. "Hang on one second."

Unable to resist, I ground gently down on the hard bulge straining against his pants, eliciting a groan from Deus.

He brought me around the side of the bookcase and into his makeshift bedroom. My jaw dropped. Deus hadn't been lying. His bed *was* pretty interesting.

For one thing, it hovered three feet in the air. And for another, it was made of clouds.

"How do you do this?" I asked breathlessly as he set me down on the top.

It was like fluffy cotton, and I'd never felt a softer mattress in my life. Above us, a miniature cloud shone like the sun was just behind it. Next to the bed sat a nightstand with a novel and a glass of water.

Deus kneeled. "A couple of solidity spells. I'll warn you, after an hour, you might be a little too warm. I usually sleep naked."

Now *that* was a sight I could wake up to.

Deus put one hand on each knee, then looked up at me, his eyes wide pools of blue. "Can I taste you?"

"Um." Every drop of liquid in my body rushed between my thighs. "Yes?"

Deus ran a tongue over his lips and a full body shiver traveled through me. He reached up, gently pulling down my sweatpants, followed by my thong.

Taking off my shirt, I lay back and watched Deus settle himself between my legs.

A few hours ago, I would have been more likely to slap Deus rather than having sex with him. But he'd stood up to Ezric for me, and then he'd told me how much I meant to him… and now all I wanted to do was feel his touch and to touch him back.

Deus' lips kissed just above my knee and moved steadily north. His tongue swirled on the sensitive skin of my thigh, and I made a strangled sound.

He paused. "Are you all right?"

"Why did you stop?" I gasped.

He chuckled. "I'll take that to mean you're fine. Seta? You can take your cuff off, if you want. You're safe here."

Then he disappeared between my legs and neither of us could speak. I couldn't have strung together a sentence if I'd wanted, and his mouth was otherwise occupied.

His tongue swirled, licked, sucked, and explored all my sensitive places, pushing me to the edge of my climax, only to back off at the last moment. It was a rapturous type of torture.

"Please, Deus," I begged, my body vibrating with the need for release.

I was lost to the cool softness of the bed, the heat of his mouth on my clit, the shivers that chased each other over my skin. Again, he brought me to the very edge, but this time, he kept going, finally allowing my release.

I cried out in pleasure as I came, the need that had coiled painfully tight burst free sending pleasure surging through me. A gentle rainstorm broke above me, splattering my skin with soft, warm drops.

## KRAMMIN' WITH A KRAKEN

Breathing hard, I looked down. Our eyes met over my stomach. His mouth was still firmly attached to my clit.

During my orgasm, I'd lost control of my shift, and my tentacles were wrapped around his chest. His eyes crinkled, and I knew he was smiling. Then his tongue flicked over my clit, and my head fell back against the bed as I was lost to the world again.

After my second orgasm, he broke away and crawled up to me.

"I don't think I can do another round with your tentacles undressing and teasing me," he said regretfully.

I laughed. "They kind of have a mind of their own."

Deus was poised above me, his cock pressed erect and hungry against my belly.

Tiny red circles dotted his chest and midriff, and I pressed a kiss to one. "Sorry about this. I guess I got carried away."

"Yeah, you did. But I was into it." He pressed in for a full, intoxicating kiss.

My fingers drifted down to circle the head of his cock. It was already wet. I swirled pre-cum around the tip and Deus groaned against my lips.

"Shall I return the favor?" I murmured.

"What do you want?" he asked, eyes heavy-lidded with arousal.

"Well, I owe you," I replied half-jokingly.

Deus stiffened. Shifting his weight, he took my chin in one golden hand. Glowing light pulsed from him, and the cloud over our heads turned a deep blue.

"That's not how sex works. You don't owe me anything," he said, gently but firmly. "Now, what do you *want*?"

No one had ever asked me what I wanted.

Tears blurred my vision.

My desire to go to Slaymore had conveniently coincided with my father's need for a human ambassador and my mother's desire to get me mated. I hadn't gotten to choose my project partners or even how I learned all the things I wanted to know. My parents had never asked what I wanted my future to be like.

So what did I want, right here and now?

"I want you," I murmured. "Amadeus? I think you're right. You are my mate."

Deus' face froze in surprise. "Really? You're not just saying it?"

I was terrified to admit the truth, but I was determined to stop being afraid of closeness.

"Yes. It scared me, and it's one of the reasons I pushed you away. My soul says you're mine. And there are other things—like how I'm drawn to you and how you were able to see my tattoos even though you aren't a kraken."

"I am yours, Seta. For as long as you will have me." Deus' glow was so bright I was forced to squint.

"Good. Because I want you forever." I pressed a kiss to his chest. "Now enough talking. I want you to show me what I mean to you."

Deus smiled and turned to the nightstand. With a bit of fumbling, he pulled out a condom. Staring at the flexing muscles of his bare back and the sexy lines of his body, I was struck by how much I wanted him.

*Mine.*

I wanted his body, his smile, his soft words, his gentle spirit. I *wanted* to know what it was like to wake up next to him, to sit across the table from him for breakfast.

This wasn't the plan. Falling in love used to be the type of nonsense I wanted to avoid. Now, I couldn't imagine my life without him.

Then he turned back to me, carefully positioning his body over mine. "I always thought most paranormals were incompatible in terms of, you know, conception."

"Well, my dad can make offspring without trying," he joked, then his face grew serious. "Seta, I know how important your studies are and the work you want to pursue in the Deep. I don't want to do anything to jeopardize that for you. In the future, maybe we could reconsider things."

My throat tightened with a swell of emotions. Even in the heat of the moment, Deus was protecting my dreams and taking care of me. Before I could respond, the head of his cock bumped against my slit. A moment later, he pressed into my body, effectively ending further conversation.

When we'd been in the water, I'd been in charge. But now we were in Deus' domain. He moved slowly, as though he wanted to experience every moment to its fullest.

Electricity flickered between his fingers and crackled down his arms. It shot into the cloud bed, and a stray bolt zapped across my shoulder. I tensed, but not from pain. No, the stinging kiss of his lightning had added to my excitement.

Above us, the little cloud flashed with intra-cloud lightning.

Deus gasped. "Sorry. Control is something I've struggled with the past twenty-four hours."

"It's okay." I smirked up at him. "I'm kind of into it."

With a rumble of laughter, Deus dropped his head to kiss my neck and his hips thrust forward. A shock jumped from his skin to mine, causing me to tense again and Deus' cock to twitch.

Slowly, he withdrew, then thrust again, kissed again. It became a pattern—thrust, kiss, shock. My pleasure began to rise, building with each surge of electricity.

I forced myself not to wrap myself around him and speed up the pace like my body was demanding. No, I wanted him to take his time. I wanted him to be in control of our pleasure.

For several minutes, the only sounds were that of needy whimpers and moans. Lightning crackled around us, and the scent of smoke tickled my nose.

I should have been afraid that he would lose control and turn me into kraken calamari, but the danger only added to my excitement. With each pump of his hips, I was getting closer to the edge.

He thrust forward once more, sending a surge of lightning licking across my overly sensitive skin, and I cried out, my orgasm swallowing me like a tidal wave. My walls tightened, milking his cock, and that sent him over the edge.

Deus' thighs trembled and his arms slipped behind my back. Intense heat and blinding light blazed from his body. The cloud above us broke again, and the falling raindrops sizzled as they hit his skin.

His face was screwed up, his eyes shut tight.

I tugged a hand through his hair, still panting from the force of my climax. "Deus?"

"I'm all right." He blinked, and lightning flashed through his eyes. When he blinked again, they were gone.

Flopping down next to me, Deus pulled me close and laughed. "Actually, I'm much better than all right."

I didn't know how to respond to that, but then he was kissing me gently, so I didn't have to. My thoughts started to drift as the chaos of the past two days caught up with me.

My eyes grew heavy. I was so tired, and curling into the warmth of Deus' comforting heat was the perfect way to fall asleep.

He was perfect.

Smart, kind, gorgeous, and just plain perfect.

*You didn't come here to fall in love*, whispered the sensible voice lurking in the back of my mind.

*Too late*, I thought back groggily.

# CHAPTER 19
## SETA

The rest of the semester went by in a blur. Now that I was Deus' girlfriend, Ayla told me I had to participate in friend group stuff, so I'd been pushing to do things outside my comfort zone… like interacting with people.

It was slightly easier, since I no longer had to look at Ezric's smirking face. Somehow, the entire experience of other people was much more pleasant without him. I wasn't the only one. Jenny had whispered her thanks that Ezric wasn't around anymore as well.

"I'm so glad he listened to you. He wouldn't listen to any of us." She tilted her chin in Deus' direction. "He's too busy trying to be angelic, and he struggles to see anything but the good in others."

I didn't answer. Just the mention of Ezric made me tense up and reach for my cuff.

That guy knew both too little and too much about me, and the fact that he'd stayed quiet about my secret had me nervous he was planning something.

According to Jenny, Ezric had sported a black eye and busted lip after leaving Deus' apartment. She was convinced that Deus had been the cause of Ezric's mangled face, but I couldn't imagine my too-nice-for-his-own-good Labrador of a boyfriend raising a fist to anyone... no matter how much they deserved it.

I thought of the tooth in Ezric's hand, still flaked with the blood of my brethren. Suddenly, my food tasted like mud. Trying to shove the thought of him out of my mind, I glanced around the table at the smiling faces.

Bianca must have figured out that something was bothering me, because she shot me a quizzical look. I gave her what I hoped was a reassuring smile in return. She and I had spent time together at *Spellcaster's* sipping on Sassy Seniors, while she quizzed me about various transformation signs until I'd felt ready for finals.

I thankfully survived the alchemy exam, aced basic incantations, and I'd already turned in my final academic writing paper.

I had no real reason to be nervous, but I couldn't help but pick at my food. Moirus had invited us to dine in the lycanthrope hall that evening—Tatiana was a werewolf, apparently—and listening to them bicker over their study notes made it difficult for me to get my anxiety under control. I doubted I'd be able to eat while my stomach was so jittery.

"You don't have to be here," Deus murmured, sitting next to me and sliding over until our thighs were flush against each other.

"Yes, I do. I heard it would make my boyfriend happy," I quipped, fighting the urge to shift and wrap my tentacles around him.

I'd gone from being a loner in the sea to becoming the world's most clingy girlfriend... literally.

Deus grinned. "I think 'boyfriend' is the sexiest word ever to come out of your mouth." He pressed his lips to mine.

Something flat and wet smacked our faces. Numina had thrown a piece of lettuce. "It should be illegal to be so smoochy while we are in the midst of panic study time," she grouched.

Deus squeezed my knee, and I laughed. Somehow, I felt well enough to eat a bit after all.

"Is there anything you *would* consider attending with me?" Deus asked with an exaggerated smile on his face.

We stood in his kitchenette, finally making time for a study session with just the two of us.

"It's just that when everyone's busy partying Friday

night, the library's perfectly quiet," I whined, moving to his side and going up on tip-toe to plant a kiss on his cheek. "And Saturday morning after a party is even better."

I loved studying, and even if my future had shifted to include the possibility of having a mate, I wasn't willing to let go of my dreams.

"People are accusing me of making you up when I tell them I have a girlfriend. You better be careful... one day some siren might set her sights on me," Deus teased, his eyes glinting with amusement.

One tentacle slipped out of its enchantment and down the back of his jeans. I nipped his neck and whispered, "Yeah, and you'll turn her down."

Our banter turned into a short tussle of remove-the-pants, and somehow our assignments were forgotten.

When we'd gotten control of ourselves and were dressing for dinner, Deus asked, "How about tonight? We are going to play a movie on a projector on the main lawn, kind of like a drive-in, but without the cars. Everyone at Slaymore is going to be there."

"You do realize this is the last week to study before finals week, right?" I asked while triple-checking my cuff.

I'd noticed it half off one night when I was sneaking back to my dorm room, and had thanked Poseidon that Ezric hadn't ambushed me with another spell. Now I'd become a bit paranoid about checking and double-checking it.

Deus put on a sea-green shirt that made his eyes appear as blue as the Caribbean Ocean. "A lot of students leave right after their last final, so it's the last time everyone will be together before January. Jenny will be there. And Bianca."

I'd grown fond of Jenny and Bianca. "Good. They'll keep any ravaging sirens off you."

I expected him to laugh his easy going laugh that made my stomach flutter, but his shoulders sagged instead.

My eyes shot to his face. Deus was serious about this.

I chewed my lip as I searched for my tights, which had been flung to goddess knew where in the heat of the moment. If going to a party meant that much to Deus, then surely I could suck it up for one night.

"Fine. I'll come. That way, I can make sure all those girls keep their hands to themselves."

*Because I definitely didn't plan to keep my hands to myself.*

SHIVERING, I LEANED BACK AGAINST DEUS' chest. The movie was only a third of the way through and I was already bored.

We didn't have movies in the Deep, and I struggled to figure out why people enjoyed them. I preferred a book over a movie any day of the week.

"Are you cold?" Deus whispered next to my ear, even though the nearest couple was several meters in front of us, and unlikely to hear him.

The lawn was scattered with students lying on blankets and sitting in portable lawn chairs. The night was dark, but I could easily see around me thanks to my kraken abilities.

"A little," I whispered back, cuddling deeper into the warmth of his arms.

Deus grabbed an extra blanket he'd brought and tucked it around us. "Better?"

Instead of answering, I turned my head to place a kiss on his stubbled jawline. Deus' eyes stayed glued to the screen, but I didn't miss the added warmth he radiated.

A tendril of need blossomed deep in my belly, and an intriguing idea drifted through my mind. I touched the cuff on my wrist. It would keep me from losing control and shifting completely... but did I dare risk being seen?

Desire won over logic.

I allowed just my legs to shift to tentacles beneath the blanket, and kept my movements slow so that Deus might not suspect anything right away. With that finished, I reached for his hand. Sliding it under the hem of my shirt, I moved it upward until he cupped my aching breast.

We both groaned, and sitting between his legs, I could easily feel his erection twitch against my backside.

"What are you doing, Seta?" Deus growled, sucking and nipping at my neck.

I didn't answer. Instead, my tentacle slithered up his thigh. Deus was wearing sweats, so it was easy to slip inside his pants. When the feathered tip of my tentacle brushed his length, Deus sucked in a sharp breath.

"You've got to stop," he rumbled, even as his fingers

made their way beneath my bra to tease the hardened peak of my nipple.

Coiling my tentacle around his quickly hardening cock, I purposely positioned one of my suckers right on the tip. As I began to stroke, I used the cup to provide a unique suction.

Deus' body shuddered, and I could feel his heart pounding against my back.

"If you aren't going to stop, it's only fair we both enjoy this." Deus' fingers trailed downward, moving from my breast to the band of my skirt.

"Oh, I am enjoying myself," I purred, arching away from him a little to give the tentacle pumping him more room to work.

Deus sucked at the tender flesh between my shoulder and my neck. "Not as much as you enjoyed yourself that night in the pond."

I stiffened. "What do you mean?"

His deep laughter sent liquid rushing between my legs. "Do you really think I don't know what you were doing beneath the water, naughty girl?"

My entire body flushed with embarrassment, and I was thankful it was dark. "I, uh... I—"

"It was one of those times I felt your emotions. And do you know what I felt?" His fingers slipped beneath the band of my skirt.

"N-no?" My breathing was coming in short gasps, humiliation and lust fighting for dominance inside me.

"Need. I thought you were hurt and needed help. It

wasn't until I got to the pond and tried to help you from the water that I realized what type of need you were experiencing."

He'd known. I thought I'd been so smooth, but Deus had known.

I begged for the ground to open up and swallow me.

"I nearly came apart when I realized you were pleasuring yourself while thinking of me... but then you did something I never expected. You kept going. I didn't miss the way the water rocked with your movements, or how stunning your bedroom eyes were. Then you orgasmed right there in front of me and it was the most beautiful thing I'd ever seen."

I whimpered and tried to cover my burning face with my hands.

Deus' fingers brushed along my soaked slit. "Do you know how many times I've jacked off to that memory? How many times I have tried to imagine exactly how you were touching yourself beneath the water?"

"Deus, please. I can't believe I did that. It's not like me!"

He slipped a single finger inside me. "Then why did you do it?"

"Because I was constantly feeling drawn to you. My body longed for your touch, and I thought if I could let off some steam, I could keep things professional between us," I hissed.

"You wanted me." Deus sounded proud.

"Yes. I wanted you so much it was hard to think. My plan didn't include finding a mate—I mean, boyfriend—but

I hadn't planned on meeting you." I gently squeezed his rock-hard cock, and Deus thrust into my tentacle.

"After seeing you transform in the lake, I began to wonder if it was possible you hadn't been in your human form in the pond. It's been driving me crazy not knowing." Deus slipped a second finger inside me. "Seta, were you using your tentacle to pleasure yourself?"

I didn't answer.

Deus pulled his fingers from my aching core, leaving me empty. "Seta..."

"Please," I begged, wanting his touch, but not wanting to admit to my shameless behavior in the pond.

"Did you ride your tentacle while I held your arm? Did it turn you on more knowing I was right there?" he pressed, teasing me.

Despite my embarrassment, there was something about hearing how much he'd been affected that night that was turning me on.

"Yes. I'd never done anything like that, and it was one of the hottest things I'd ever experienced," I answered, my voice husky.

Deus groaned and dropped his head against my shoulder. Tiny lightning bolts streaked across his skin as he struggled to control himself.

I fought the urge to slip my hand between my thighs, desperately needing to be touched.

"Show me." Deus's voice was raw.

"Huh?" I asked, confused.

His hand slid across the tentacle that wasn't busy

stroking him. "I want you to do it again. But this time, I want to control your tentacle."

My body trembled, but beneath the blanket, I placed the end of my free tentacle in his palm. "Okay."

Deus' cock seemed to grow thicker in my grasp. He was excited.

He pressed the feathered tip of my tentacle against my entrance, slowly pushing it inside. I gasped.

"Seta, I want you to press one of your suckers against your clit, just like you're doing on the head of my cock." He growled the order against my neck, and I quickly obeyed.

Deus' fingers moved to explore, making sure I'd done as he said. "Good girl."

I nearly fell apart right then. "Deus? I'm not going to last long."

"Neither am I." Deus was rocking hard against the tentacle coiling and moving along his hardened length.

His hand worked the end of my tentacle, the edge of the suction cups providing the friction I desperately craved.

"You're mine." Deus' breathing was ragged.

He was right. I was his, and he was mine.

I knew to the depths of my soul that there would never be anyone else for me. Deus was my other half. He'd been gifted to me by the Fates. My future still had a lot of unknowns, but Deus wasn't one of them.

He was part of my future... and the rest of my life.

*I loved him.*

"Yes. I'm yours."

My imprints blazed to life, and pleasure erupted inside

me, searing my mind and body with sensations so powerful I couldn't breathe or move. I was completely silent as I came apart in Deus' arms.

Behind me, Deus thrust one final time against my tentacle. His cock began to jerk in my hold, as he spilled the evidence of his own desire.

As the roar in my ears quieted, and my vision began to clear, my focus landed on my arms.

"Those are beautiful. You told me that krakens gain imprints as something happens in their life, right?" Deus asked, hooking his chin over my shoulder and pulling me close.

"Yes." I was trying not to hyperventilate.

Krakens gained their imprints when something life-changing happened in their lives. Saving a life, stopping a tsunami, sinking a warship...

The imprints never ceased appearing, and an old kraken could be completely covered in the swirling lines and ancient script. It allowed us, and other krakens, to see the proud history of our lives as guardians of the sea.

Deus traced one of the lines that still retained some of the red glow. "This one is new. What does it represent?"

"It shows that I took a mate."

I wasn't sure Deus had heard me until he turned me in his arms so that I straddled his lap.

He caught my face between his palms. "Are you saying we're mated?"

"Krakens mate for life. I can't undo it, Amadeus." Tears

streamed down my cheeks and my heart attempted to pound through my ribcage.

"Good." Deus placed a soft kiss on my lips. "Now you're stuck with me."

I leaned back. "You're not upset?"

Deus laughed. "Seta, you're the one who wanted to be casual. I agreed because I was willing to be anything you wanted me to be… as long as I could be with you. Hades, I would've been thrilled if you'd taken me as your mate that very first day."

Fresh tears slid down my cheeks. "I love you, my mate."

Lightning crackled overhead, and the boom of thunder sent several students shrieking toward the main buildings. Rain kissed my skin as Deus leaned forward to press another kiss against my lips.

"I love you, Seta. I can't believe I'm lucky enough to have you as my mate."

Our lips met in a kiss filled with passion, love, and excitement for our future.

# CHAPTER 20
## SETA

The marine mythology final was set for nine that evening. In my human form, I was still susceptible to cold air, so I put on my puffy winter coat and headed out to the lake at 8:45. The night was clear and bright, with a full moon smiling down on us.

My breath frosted in the air as I joined the line of students at the edge of the lake. We stood near the rocks on the deep end, studying the lights twinkling beneath the surface of the lake.

Deus moved to stand next to me. He was dressed in a simple hoodie, and radiated confidence and heat.

"Koidos," barked Mackenzie from the edge of the lake. He looked a little peeved. "You're going to have to tone it down."

Deus looked at his hands. "How am I supposed to keep

warm?"

"You've got a coat, I presume? Otherwise, you can freeze. You're calling out the sea-wights."

I grimaced. "You'd better go get a coat."

I was a kraken, and even I didn't want to risk tangling with sea-wights. They were such nasty little creatures.

Deus gave me a single, searing kiss on the lips before he jogged off. I smiled as I watched him go. The smile dimmed a little as I realized I'd have to tell my mother I'd gotten a boyfriend.

I'd have to physically restrain her from running off to toll the giant bell that signaled celebrations in the Deep. Mother and Father would want to meet him, of course, which would require some pretty big transformation spells—

A rough hand grabbed my arm, jerking me from my thoughts.

"Hey—" I began, but before I could finish my protest, a second hand closed around my cuff and ripped it off, hard enough that it sliced the skin on my wrist.

"Now that your protector is gone, let's see the real you," Ezric snarled in my ear.

He gave me a vicious shove that sent me toppling off the rocky ledge.

The water enveloped me like home, and my body began to unfurl from its enchantment.

*No,* I thought, flailing in panic. But I'd been in human form for so long, and part of me was so tired of it that my resistance was feeble.

## KRAMMIN' WITH A KRAKEN

I tried to at least keep a semi-shifted form, but the fear, anger, and anxiety coursing through me made it impossible to focus and gain control.

Despite my best efforts, my arms lengthened and transformed. Rows of powerful suckers sprouted along their length. My legs did the same, quickly reaching out to find the bottom of the lake and stabilizing me.

In this form, I was the size of a small house. My dark tentacles with their fire-red feathery tips slithered through the water, while my glowing alien-esque eyes took in the scene unfolding in front of me.

People shrieked and the scene on shore reminded me of the stupid B-rated shark movies Deus was so fond of watching.

Someone screamed, "Oh my gods, is that part of the final?"

"Are we under attack?" screamed another.

Professor Mackenzie gaped at me from where he stood, waist-deep in water and surrounded by various saltwater creatures.

A single word traveled around the lake, passed from student to student.

*Kraken.*

So much for keeping a low profile.

*Suck my life.*

My first instinct was to duck beneath the water. If I could keep my tentacles hidden, maybe Headmistress Losia and I could find a way to spin this. Maybe we could call me some kind of giant octopus-shifter. Only Mackenzie would know there was no such thing, and he might be willing to keep my secret.

"Come out, Seta. Fight me like the monster you are."

The rectangular pupils of my eyes adjusted quickly, allowing me to see Ezric as clearly as if it were daytime.

The slayer hoisted his harpoon gun, leveling it at me.

Several students gasped and threw themselves away from him. The creatures of the lake recognized the harpoon gun, and beneath the water, they thrashed about with terror and turmoil.

But I wasn't a monster.

I was a shepherd of the sea.

A protector.

One tentacle flicked out, comforting a small greentooth and a miniature sea drake.

*I won't let him hurt you,* I thought, allowing the water to carry my words to them.

"Seta." Professor Mackenzie's arms were up, and his face was as pale as the moon.

There was a tremor of fear in his voice, and my heart twisted. Even my favorite professor was afraid of me, and that knowledge made me want to cry.

"It'll be alright. Why don't you come out of the water?" Mackenzie coaxed in the same way you'd try to calm a rabid wolf.

The harpoon gun flashed. A bolt arced over the water, flashing with spells.

Without thinking, I drew on the saltwater, creating a

wave that rose up and caught the bolt. Green flashed like lightning within the wave as a spell activated on impact.

I snatched the bolt with one tentacle and flung it into the air before a second spell could detonate. The bolt exploded, showering wood and steel down on the lake.

I snatched a fragment away from a curious bottom feeder even as several pieces of the falling steel sliced across my skin.

"You're quick on your feet— Oh, sorry. Is that a sore subject?" Ezric mocked.

"Not at all." My voice reverberated through the air, like a whale song through the water. I was proud of how calm I sounded, since I'd never been more scared in my life. "I love my body."

With slow, deliberate movements, I swam away from the side of the lake where Mackenzie and the students stood. The farther I was from them, the safer they would be.

"Why wouldn't you?" He reached into his pocket. "You could kill all of us, couldn't you?"

Could I grab him with my tentacle? From the corner of my eye, I saw the bright light of someone's phone. They were recording this. Which meant if I picked him up, I'd look like every single evil kraken ever to grace a landlubber's nightmare or television.

"That's not what Poseidon made us for," I replied. "I'm a protector."

"Liar!" he shouted, his breath coming in hard gasps and his eyes shining with a deranged fervor. "You had to sneak into Slaymore because you *knew* that no one would accept your kind. You don't belong. You're a threat to all living things."

Ezric threw something at me.

A grenade.

Throwing up another watery wall, I blocked it before it could sink beneath the water's surface and injure the terrified creatures darting about. The grenade bounced off the watery shield and landed among the huddled students.

Ezric didn't seem to notice, or maybe he just didn't care. I lunged toward land, my tentacle stretching out to snatch the grenade. Just as I wrapped my thick tentacle around it, Ezric fired the harpoon.

Fiery pain surged through my tentacle, but I refused to drop the grenade. With the harpoon sticking out from my appendage, there was no way I could fling the grenade far enough to clear the academy buildings.

That left one choice.

Coiling my tentacle tightly around the weapon, I braced myself.

I roared in agony as it exploded and hundreds of tiny metal shards pierced my sensitive skin. Students scrambled away from me, fear etched across their stark faces.

Pulling my injured tentacle back into the water, I sunk down beneath the surface. Gritting my teeth, I yanked the pointed tip out of my skin.

Krakens had healing abilities, but I couldn't start healing until the weapon was removed. This injury was going to take a while to heal, judging by the blood spilling into the water around me.

## KRAMMIN' WITH A KRAKEN

"Monster! Show yourself or I'll slice her throat!" Ezric's voice traveled through the water.

Ignoring the pain still ricocheting through my body, I pushed myself off the lake floor. I burst out of the water, waves crashing to shore around me with a snarl that sent rocks tumbling into the lake.

Hades knew I was trying to be patient, but with each attack on the innocents around him, it was becoming more difficult to keep from becoming the monster he wanted me to be.

"You are just as soft as that boyfriend of yours!" Ezric taunted.

The slayer held a tearful Jenny in front of him, a knife pressed to her neck. My tentacles glowed as fury bubbled in me like molten lava.

"Stand down!" Mackenzie barked, finally convinced that I wasn't going to lash out at him. He waded toward shore, brandishing a finger at Ezric. "Stand down *now*. Release Jenny and relinquish your weapons—"

"Oh, shut up, old man!" Ezric snarled, using his free hand to hurl a tiny metal sphere at the professor.

The spell ball hit Mackenzie mid-stride and broke open, allowing the spell to flow out. Instantly, the professor froze. An immobility spell.

My world slowed to a crawl, even as my mind raced. If the spell ball hit the water, who knew how many of the water-dwelling creatures it would freeze, or what would happen to them. Many needed to come up for oxygen periodically, and being held immobile beneath the water would cause them to drown.

Mackenzie began to pitch forward, his eyes rolling in terror as he tumbled face-first into the water. He disappeared beneath the surface, unable to move to save himself from drowning.

Ezric turned away from the professor, not caring that the man could be dying, and focused his attention back on me.

Knowing the cost of what I was about to do, I called on the ancient magic of the Deep that flowed through my veins. I was faster and stronger than any creature in the ocean. Even on land, my only equal was a dragon.

Ezric's family had only survived their hunts because krakens tended to be gentle with other species, knowing how easy it was for us to harm someone accidentally.

We understood that the people who encountered us were likely terrified, therefore we paid no mind to their efforts to defend themselves with human weapons. But that put us at a disadvantage when we encountered a hunter because they came armed with the weapons that could kill us, and by the time we realized their purpose, it was often too late.

I lashed out with my tentacles. The first found Mackenzie, lifting him out of the water. Using a second, I wrenched the knife from Ezric's grasp and slammed it hilt deep into the tree behind him.

At the same time, I used a third tentacle to snatch Jenny away from the slayer. Pulling her into the water, I hid her trembling body behind me.

With a fourth, I caught the metal ball, causing the spell to flow up my body instead of harming the creatures in the lake. I'd barely managed to brace my leg tentacles to the bottom of the lake before I, too, was frozen.

The spell, Mackenzie, and Jenny were all safely in my grasp. Krakens were guardians, and I'd done what Poseidon had created me to do.

I stared at Ezric in defiance. *This* was what I was.

I'd come to Slaymore to prove krakens weren't monsters and that we could live among other paranormals. Even if I died at Ezric's hand, I would have accomplished what I'd set out to do.

But I was sort of hoping that *someone* would step in before he murdered me.

Ezric raised the harpoon gun. "I have to say, this was disappointingly easy. My family always made your type out to be so tough. All those years Uncle Jonas spent puffing himself up—maybe he just lied about the whole thing to make the hunt sound more exciting. Ah, well." He raised a sardonic eyebrow. "Either way, it'll make good conversation around my family's Christmas tree this year."

An ear-splitting *crack* rent the air. For a brief yet terrifying moment, I thought the harpoon gun had gone off, and that crack signified my life was coming to an end. But then the thickest column of lightning I'd ever seen lit up the edge of the lake. The lightning retreated, leaving a blazing white figure behind.

Ezric fell to his knees, his mouth dropping open, and the harpoon gun sagged at his side. The students huddled together on the other side of the lake as the shining figure moved forward.

*Deus.*

He was brighter than I'd ever seen him. And it wasn't the bright glow of happiness or security. *Oh no.*

For the first time ever, I witnessed the blaze of Deus' fury. With each step he took, the grass underfoot combusted and left blackened prints as he approached Ezric. He was so bright it seared my eyes to look at him.

Even from a distance, I could see Ezric trembling. The slayer was so completely transfixed by terror he was unable to move or fight.

Reaching down and careful not to touch skin to skin, Deus removed the harpoon gun from Ezric's unresisting grip. Electricity sizzled over the gun and something inside it popped, while the outer casing melted and began to drip onto the scorched grass.

Satisfied it was useless, Deus tossed the harpoon to the ground. I watched in awe as he rolled his shoulders, took a deep breath, and dimmed his glow. Deus still radiated light, but now he shone more like the moon—bright, but no longer painful to look at.

He leaned over Ezric and pulled things from the slayer's belt. A hunting knife, a spell book, a net. Then he pulled a fishing spear from a holster on Ezric's back. And one by one, he destroyed them. He warped the knife blade, burned the book with a single touch, tore the net, and bent the harpoon with ease.

"You need to leave." Deus' tone was uncompromising.

Ezric's mouth worked, and his tongue darted out to wet his lips. "Have you *seen* her? Even Mackenzie was terrified. She's a monster! And a liar! How else did she get admitted? No one would want to attend Slaymore if they knew! She's a threat!"

"Maybe the most threatening thing at Slaymore isn't a mythical monster, but the slayer who thinks his desires are more important than another being's right to live." Deus' voice was low, both soft and lethal at the same time.

Any other time, it would have been a turn on...

Who was I trying to kid? I was definitely getting turned on by this new side of my mate.

Reaching down, he pulled Ezric up by the arm, none too gently, and turned him away.

Ezric spun around. "You can't do this! Think, Deus. My family, you know what they'll do to me. And for what? Your tentacle-toy is going to be expelled anyway—"

Deus' fist moved in a glimmering blur. The resounding crack as it connected with Ezric's face echoed across the lake.

Ezric reeled away, clutching his bloody nose. "What the—?"

Deus stood straight, blue lightning crackling around him. "That was a warning. Don't ever talk about my mate with disrespect again. Next time, I won't be so gentle."

There were soft gasps from the students and faculty who'd rushed to the lake, but I didn't know if it was due to the shock of hearing the sweetest guy on campus threaten someone, or if it was because Deus had called me his mate.

Deus handed Ezric off to two of the professors who'd noticed the commotion and come to investigate. As they escorted Ezric to Headmistress Losia's office, Deus moved to the edge of the lake.

"Seta? You're safe. I'd come to you, but right now I'm afraid I'll lose control and fry everything in the lake."

I rolled my eyes.

One of the students on the shore cleared their throat. "Ezric used an immobility spell on her."

"Zeus! Someone take it off!" he snarled.

There was more muttering, and then a flash of light came from within the student huddle. A moment later, the tips of my tentacles began to tingle as feeling and control returned to my limbs.

Moving closer to shore, I carefully lowered Professor Mackenzie to the ground, keeping the tentacle around him until he stood on his own. "That's quite sufficient. I appreciate the help," he rumbled.

Sighing in relief, I let them sag back beneath the water.

With the immediate threat gone, I slowly studied the faces lining the shore.

Everyone was staring at me, and most had their phones out. Summoning as much dignity as I could muster, I brought myself to the edge of the lake.

It took some effort, but I managed to transform two tentacles back into my legs so I could walk on land. Then I shifted two tentacles back to arms, but let the other four fan out around me.

Then, without hesitating, I walked up to Deus and

kissed him. My tentacles wrapped around his chest and waist as I clung to my mate.

*There*. Let them take a picture of that.

"That's my bestie!" Ayla's voice rose above the din of students talking.

I rolled my eyes, ignoring her, and focusing on Deus' lips against mine.

He was warm.

So warm that the water evaporated from my skin in little waves of steam.

So warm that I had to break away. "Ow."

"Sorry." Deus took another deep breath, bringing his glow to an almost normal level. He cupped my cheek. "Are you all right?"

I thought about it. "I guess that depends on what happens to Ezric. What if they let him off the hook?" I hesitated, then added, "And I guess it depends on whether he was right."

Would the rest of the students make an uproar about my presence at Slaymore? Would they campaign for me to be expelled? Would I have to go back home and give up on my dreams, or would I spend the rest of my education looking over my shoulder for enemies? I didn't even know which option was worse.

"Ezric's going to be expelled."

I jumped.

Professor Mackenzie had snuck up behind us. "Attacking a student unprovoked? Attacking a teacher? Sabotaging his final exam? There are a lot of ways to get him out of here. And I will personally stand for you against every disgruntled bigot who even thinks about complaining. Slaymore was the first paranormal educational institution to admit dragons, succubi, gryphons and gorgons, and we'll be proud to add krakens to the list."

He cupped his hands around his mouth and roared at the students. "The marine mythology final is postponed until after the break. I'm sure you all see why. Your grades will be marked as incomplete until you've taken the final." He dropped his hands, then said to me in a normal voice, "You get an A."

"But..." I flushed, pride warring with my sense of justice. "But I didn't take the final."

"Seta, you've never gotten below a 93 on my assignments. I think we can assume you'd have done well here."

A student came running up to us. "Headmistress Losia's asking for you." She was looking everywhere but at me.

"We'd best not keep her waiting." Mackenzie started across the lawn.

Deus bent and picked up my cuff, holding it out. "You don't have to, but if you want to..."

"I don't, and I'm tired of keeping the secret. Besides, everyone on campus will know by tomorrow." I waved a tentacle at the cellphones still pointed in my direction. "It's time for me to show the world I'm not ashamed of being a kraken, and that we aren't to be feared."

Deus grinned. "That's my girl."

## CHAPTER 21
### SETA

"You can miss the ferry, right?" Deus ran a hand through my hair.

We lay on his bed in a tangle of limbs and tentacles. His playful smile told me he was joking, even though his rapidly stiffening cock told me he was ready for another round.

I sat up with a groan. "Tomorrow's weather looks bad. Tonight is the last night I can get out. But it's only for three weeks."

I'd opted to return to Slaymore the week before class started, to move my stuff from my dorm room to Deus' room. Plus, I'd promised I'd join a club with Ayla, and we had to decide on which one.

To my dismay, when my guard had been down—thanks to an incredible orgasm—I'd promised Deus we'd do one extracurricular activity each week. And that had somehow turned into Ayla wanting us to go shopping to get me an entirely new wardrobe.

"Besides," I added, addressing the elephant in the room, "we have to plan our next political move."

Ezric had been expelled, just like Professor Mackenzie had predicted.

Headmistress Losia had written up two statements—one condemning student violence and discrimination, and one officially welcoming Slaymore's first kraken student. Amid the cheers, she'd also announced that paperwork had been filed, with the full backing of Slaymore's faculty, to pressure paranormal lawmakers to recognize Krakens as a protected species.

There would be many meetings and interviews needed to see our status changed, but it was a strong start, and I was excited to be part of making it happen... even if I was nearly killed in the process.

Ezric's family had already retaliated in the usual paranormal newspapers and interviews, but they were scrambling behind the scenes.

That the son of a high-ranking slayer family had tried to kill an ambassador from another race looked bad for all slayers, and a number of other slayer families had already reached out to the Bering clan with peace offerings. I was getting the distinct feeling that Ezric's family wasn't exactly popular among his kind.

My parents were beyond proud that I was accomplishing what they'd sent me here to do... make the world safer for krakens.

"I am sorry," I whispered.

Even though he despised Ezric's actions, I knew he mourned for the Ezric he'd known for so long... not the Ezric I'd met.

Deus looked up at me, and his hands ran up to my shoulders, setting my body alight. I couldn't believe I'd have to survive three weeks without his touch.

"You know, I think all of us were held back by what we wanted. You only wanted to study. I only wanted to make others happy. He only wanted to prove himself to his family. But we were able to move forward and grow. If Ezric had accepted Slaymore as his family, and let go of the darkness in his heart, maybe he'd still be here."

I knew my mate was smart, but it had slipped my attention that he was also wise.

"Come visit me," I blurted out before I could think better of it.

"Over break?" He curled a strand of my hair around his finger.

I was used to regretting my hasty words, but the more I thought about it, the more it felt right. My gaze fell on my imprints, and I bit back a groan. There was no way I could hide them from my eagle-eyed parents. My dad would be proud of the imprint that etched across my skin after the battle with Ezric, but my mom would be most interested in the one about my mate.

"My mother is going to lose her kelp when she sees I'm

mated. But if you can sit through her trying to plan our wedding every waking minute... then yes."

*Say yes,* I silently urged.

I hadn't realized how badly I wanted this until now, less than two hours before I was supposed to go home.

"A visit to the Deep. Where I can't use my powers or I might electrocute someone..." he said slowly, lost in thought. Then he flashed me a grin. "What the heck? I'm in."

"You promised me you'd say no when you didn't want to do something," I reminded him, putting a hand on his chest.

Deus' heart beat a little faster than normal.

He closed his hand over mine. "I said *yes,* and I meant it. I know you'll protect me. Give me a week at home to deal with a few things, and you break the news that you have a mate to your mom, then I'll meet you at the surface to do the transformation spell. Deal?"

"Deal." I threw myself at him, my tentacles curling around his warm, muscular body.

I still had an hour before I needed to get dressed for the ferry... *that's plenty of time.*

# ABOUT DARCI R. ACULA

Darci R. Acula is Sedona Ashe's not-so-secret pen name. Sedona's books tend to focus on Reverse Harem relationships, while Darci's books feature only MF relationships.

Darci (aka Sedona) doesn't reserve her sarcasm for her books; her poor husband can tell you that her wit, humor, and snarky attitude are just part of her daily life. While she loves writing paranormal shifter reverse harem novels, she's a sucker for true love, twisted situations, and wacky humor.

Darci lives in a small town at the base of the Great Smoky Mountains in Tennessee. She and her husband share their home with their three children, adorable pup, five cats, pet arctic fox, chickens, several crazy turkeys, two chubby frogs, and over a hundred other reptiles. When she isn't working, she enjoys getting away from the computer to hike, free dive, travel, study languages, and capture images of places and animals through her photography. Darci has a crazy goal of writing a million words in a year, and spending six months exploring Indonesia.

You can find more information about the author and her books here:

www.authorsedonaashe.com
www.instagram.com/sedonaashe
www.facebook.com/sedonaashe

Find more Starling Dax books here-
www.starlingdax.com

Printed in Poland
by Amazon Fulfillment
Poland Sp. z o.o., Wrocław

35243508R00151